HQ755.8 .P3786 2014

Parenting

DATE DUE

TEEN RIGHTS AND FREEDOMS

| Parenting

TEEN RIGHTS AND FREEDOMS

I Parenting

David Haugen and Susan Musser
Book Editors

GREENHAVEN PRESS
A part of Gale, Cengage Learning

GALE
CENGAGE Learning·

Farmington Hills, Mich • San Francisco • New York • Waterville, Maine
Meriden, Conn • Mason, Ohio • Chicago

Elizabeth Des Chenes, *Director, Content Strategy*
Cynthia Sanner, *Publisher*
Douglas Dentino, *Manager, New Product*

© 2014 Greenhaven Press, a part of Gale, Cengage Learning

WCN: 01-100-101

Gale and Greenhaven Press are registered trademarks used herein under license.

For more information, contact:
Greenhaven Press
27500 Drake Rd.
Farmington Hills, MI 48331-3535
Or you can visit our Internet site at gale.cengage.com.

For product information and technology assistance, contact us at:

Gale Customer Support, 1-800-877-4253.
For permission to use material from this text or product, submit all requests online at www.cengage.com/permissions.

Further permissions questions can be emailed to permissionrequest@cengage.com.

Articles in Greenhaven Press anthologies are often edited for length to meet page requirements. In addition, original titles of these works are changed to clearly present the main thesis and to explicitly indicate the author's opinion. Every effort is made to ensure the Greenhaven Press accurately reflects the original intent of the authors. Every effort has been made to trace the owners of copyrighted material.

Cover Image © Iakov Filimonov/ShutterStock.com.

LIBRARY OF CONGRESS CATALOGING-IN-PUBLICATION DATA

Parenting / David Haugen and Susan Musser, book editors.
    pages cm. -- (Teen rights and freedoms)
    Includes bibliographical references and index.
    ISBN 978-0-7377-7001-8 (hardcover)
    1. Parenting. 2. Children's rights. I. Haugen, David M., 1969- editor of compilation. II. Musser, Susan, editor of compilation.
    HQ755.8.P3786 2014
    649'.1--dc23

                                                    2013042625

Printed in the United States of America
1 2 3 4 5 6 7 18 17 16 15 14

Contents

   The US Supreme Court's Decision

   Harry Blackmun

   The US Supreme Court finds that a parent's custodial rights can only be revoked by the state if the state follows due process procedures and can prove with clear and convincing evidence that the parent is unfit.

   The New Jersey Superior Court's Decision

   Carmen Messano

   In this state ruling, the judge finds that the minor mother's right to maintain custody of her child can be overruled by her inability to provide a safe and suitable environment in which to raise that child.

   The Kansas Supreme Court's Decision

   Richard Winn Holmes

   The Kansas State Supreme Court rules that a teen father is responsible for making child support payments to help raise his child, regardless of his age or the circumstances under which the child was conceived.

A young mother who became pregnant in high school re-counts the difficulty of returning to school after her daughter's birth due to the bullying she faced not from other students, but from teachers and school staff.

An assistant to a public school superintendent writes that teen mothers should not forsake their education, because academic training is the best path to better their lives and the lives of their children.

Some schools are initiating programs to help teenage mothers do better academically, an Associated Press writer claims. She notes how these programs monitor attendance of teen mothers, provide special classroom privileges, and even ferry homework to them if they are absent.

A woman who is close to obtaining a college degree looks back on her life and reflects that becoming pregnant at thirteen was the greatest motivator in pushing her to pursue an education. She tells of how important special assistance programs were in helping her to achieve her goals as a young, single mother.

An American author profiles one alternative high school for pregnant teens and concludes that the special attention that students receive in these schools provides the basis for more positive educational outcomes.

A journalist maintains that the closing of pregnancy schools in New York City resulted from their failure to provide separate but equal educations to the pregnant teens who attended them.

A university student insists that all high school students should be required to take parenting classes so that teens can be better informed about the best time to start a family. These courses would also teach young people about the realities of raising children and thus deter many teenagers from getting pregnant.

A school teacher worries that all the government assistance programs for pregnant teens, coupled with schools' policies that extend services to young mothers, are encouraging girls to have children, knowing that all those support services are in place to help them.

Foreword

> "In the truest sense freedom cannot be
> bestowed, it must be achieved."
> Franklin D. Roosevelt,
> September 16, 1936

The notion of children and teens having rights is a relatively recent development. Early in American history, the head of the household—nearly always the father—exercised complete control over the children in the family. Children were legally considered to be the property of their parents. Over time, this view changed, as society began to acknowledge that children have rights independent of their parents, and that the law should protect young people from exploitation. By the early twentieth century, more and more social reformers focused on the welfare of children, and over the ensuing decades advocates worked to protect them from harm in the workplace, to secure public education for all, and to guarantee fair treatment for youths in the criminal justice system. Throughout the twentieth century, rights for children and teens—and restrictions on those rights—were established by Congress and reinforced by the courts. Today's courts are still defining and clarifying the rights and freedoms of young people, sometimes expanding those rights and sometimes limiting them. Some teen rights are outside the scope of public law and remain in the realm of the family, while still others are determined by school policies.

Each volume in the Teen Rights and Freedoms series focuses on a different right or freedom and offers an anthology of key essays and articles on that right or freedom and the responsibilities that come with it. Material within each volume is drawn from a diverse selection of primary and secondary sources—journals, magazines, newspapers, nonfiction books, organization newsletters, position papers, speeches, and government documents, with a particular emphasis on Supreme Court and lower court decisions. Volumes also include first-person narratives from young people and others involved in teen rights issues, such as parents and educators. The material is selected and arranged to highlight all the major social and legal controversies relating to the right or freedom under discussion. Each selection is preceded by an introduction that provides context and background. In many cases, the essays point to the difference between adult and teen rights, and why this difference exists.

Many of the volumes cover rights guaranteed under the Bill of Rights and how these rights are interpreted and protected in regard to children and teens, including freedom of speech, freedom of the press, due process, and religious rights. The scope of the series also encompasses rights or freedoms, whether real or perceived, relating to the school environment, such as electronic devices, dress, Internet policies, and privacy. Some volumes focus on the home environment, including topics such as parental control and sexuality.

Numerous features are included in each volume of Teen Rights and Freedoms:

- An annotated **table of contents** provides a brief summary of each essay in the volume and highlights court decisions and personal narratives.

- An **introduction** specific to the volume topic gives context for the right or freedom and its impact on daily life.

- A brief **chronology** offers important dates associated with the right or freedom, including landmark court cases.

- **Primary sources**—including personal narratives and court decisions—are among the varied selections in the anthology.

- **Illustrations**—including photographs, charts, graphs, tables, statistics, and maps—are closely tied to the text and chosen to help readers understand key points or concepts.

- An annotated list of **organizations to contact** presents sources of additional information on the topic.
- A **for further reading** section offers a bibliography of books, periodical articles, and Internet sources for further research.
- A comprehensive subject **index** provides access to key people, places, events, and subjects cited in the text.

Each volume of Teen Rights and Freedoms delves deeply into the issues most relevant to the lives of teens: their own rights, freedoms, and responsibilities. With the help of this series, students and other readers can explore from many angles the evolution and current expression of rights both historic and contemporary.

Introduction

Bearing and raising a child requires a commitment that should not be taken lightly. Many couples plan for the birth of a child—stabilizing finances, establishing housing, and otherwise preparing for the difficulties and sacrifices that such a major decision entails. While adults are often responsible enough to enter into that commitment with some degree of security, teenagers typically encounter more challenges when faced with pregnancy and parenting. Like their peers, childbearing teens are coping with the demands of education, work, and social activities, but their foremost duty is to care and provide for their unborn child or newborn infant. Striking a balance is a day-to-day struggle. Unfortunately, according to the National Campaign to Prevent Teen and Unplanned Pregnancy, the statistics relating to teen parents and their children do not reflect optimistic outcomes. In its 2012 "Why It Matters? Teen Childbearing, Education, and Economic Wellbeing" factsheet, the National Campaign reports that only 38 percent of girls who give birth before they are eighteen years old acquire a high school diploma by age twenty-two. In addition, 67 percent of teen mothers who leave their families' households end up living below the poverty level. Such hardships seem to persist across successive generations, according to the organization.

Such disheartening claims are commonplace among authorities cautioning against childbirth during teen years. In 2013 the New York City Human Resources Administration (HRA) utilized similar statistics on public service posters plastered on bus stops and subway station walls, as well as on its civic social media websites. One poster displays a crying infant next to the prediction, "I'm twice as likely not to graduate high school because you had me as a teen." Another places a scowling toddler next to the warning, "Dad, you'll be paying to support me for the next 20 years." On its website, the HRA makes its intentions clear. It bluntly states, "The campaign features ads with hard-hitting facts about the money and time costs of parenting, and the negative consequences of having a child before you are ready." Some New Yorkers praise the government's strategy to make teens aware of the consequences of pregnancy. In a March 21, 2013, opinion piece for the *Daily News,* political columnist John McWhorter attests, "Shame, in reasonable dosages, can be useful. . . . We can all agree that there should be as few teenage parents as possible. All evidence is that children are better off with two parents, especially poor children. Rates of teen pregnancy have dipped since the 1990s, due to a variety of public health efforts; we should try to get them even lower." To McWhorter, teen pregnancy is a negative behavior that society irresponsibly accepts as normal; he maintains that the posters reflect obvious truths that "most of us believe, regardless of race, class or even childbearing experience."

However, not everyone believes shaming teen parents—or prospective parents—is the proper course a government should take to curb behavior. In a March 28, 2013, article for Time.com, neuroscience journalist Maia Szalavitz states that studies of the effectiveness of shaming techniques used against addicts such as alcoholics or other substance abusers have proved inconclusive. She also claims the posters put forth simple cause-and-effect relationships that in reality are much more convoluted. "The message that teen pregnancy can lead to economic hardship and a greater chance of living below the poverty level is . . . more complex than the campaign implies," Szalavitz writes. She believes the cause and effect are most likely reversed, with greater economic hardship leading to more teen pregnancies. In a March 6, 2013, press release, Haydee Morales, the vice president of education and training at New York City's Planned Parenthood, carried the argument further, blasting the government for invoking "stigma, hostility and negative public opinions about teen pregnancy and parenthood rather than offering alternative aspirations for young people." Morales argued, "The city's money would be better spent helping teens access health care, birth control and high-quality sexual and reproductive health education, not on an ad campaign intended to create shock value."

In response to a vocal public outcry, the city did make small changes to the campaign. For example, the HRA inaugurated a choose-your-own-adventure-style texting game to show interested parties the fates of two teen sweethearts who accidentally get pregnant. The HRA originally emended one text in which the young girl gets called a "fat loser" by her best friend at prom—the text now simply reads "loser." Most critics insist these minor changes do nothing to undo the kind of hurt leveled at young mothers who are already coping with stress and ostracization. One March 18, 2013, letter to the editor at the *New York Times* even chides the campaign for burdening teen mothers with the fate of their children while failing to spread the blame to young fathers adequately.

The debate over how to discourage teen pregnancy and support mothers and their children at the same time is nestled in many of the viewpoints contained in *Teen Rights and Freedoms: Parenting*. Some of the US court cases sampled herein have upheld the notion that all parents have a responsibility to raise children they have conceived; other cases included in this anthology condemn discrimination toward young parents who are trying to better their education to help provide for their children. School accommodations, welfare assistance, and other public policies aimed at helping young mothers and fathers attempt to strike that balance between achievement and sacrifice. Moreover, many of the authors make it clear that despite any public criticism of teen pregnancy, young parents have both rights and access to services that can help them move forward with their lives.

Chronology

June 1972 As part of the Education Amendments, Title IX goes into effect, stating in part that "no person in the United States shall, on the basis of sex, be excluded from participation in, be denied the benefits of, or be subjected to discrimination under any education program or activity receiving federal financial assistance."

March 1982 In *Santosky v. Kramer,* the US Supreme Court rules that the state of New York had failed to provide sufficient evidence to remove the Santosky children from their parents' home. The case affirms that state agencies seeking to separate children from their parents must definitively prove neglect.

March 1993 The Kansas Supreme Court rules in the case of *Hermesmann v. Seyer* that boys who father children while below the age of consent are still responsible for making child support payments to assist the mother in raising those children.

July 1997 The US government's Temporary Assistance for Needy Families program supplants Aid to Families with Dependent Children (AFDC) as the primary welfare aimed at families with dependent children. The states have the discretion to disburse the aid in the manner and under the restrictions they choose.

December 1998
In *Chipman v. Grant County School District,* a US district court finds that two female students in a Kentucky high school cannot be denied admittance to the institution's honor society simply because they had become pregnant. The court argues that Title IX protects against such discrimination.

May 2001
In the United States, the National Campaign to Prevent Teen and Unplanned Pregnancy sponsors the first National Day to Prevent Teen Pregnancy. The event is designed to capitalize on declining teen birth rates and make young people aware of the risks and responsibilities of teen parenting.

2008
Teen pregnancy rates in the United States drop to a forty-year low, according to the Centers for Disease Control and Prevention (CDC). A few states, however, see increases in teen pregnancy statistics from previous surveys.

June 2009
MTV begins airing *16 and Pregnant,* a reality show that follows the lives and hardships of young, pregnant girls. In December of that year, MTV launches a sister reality program, *Teen Mom,* that chronicles the lives of young mothers.

March 2012	The American Civil Liberties Union files a lawsuit on behalf of a fifteen-year-old girl who was allegedly kicked out of middle school and then humiliated at an assembly by the school director and another staff member because she was pregnant.
August 2012	In response to American Civil Liberties Union promptings, education officials in Louisiana prohibit the Delhi Charter School from denying admittance to pregnant students and mandating pregnancy tests for those suspected of being pregnant.
October 2012	In *New Jersey Division of Youth and Family Services v. L.J.D.,* a New Jersey Superior Court judge rules that the rights of the children of teenage parents to grow up in a stable, secure environment must be privileged over the rights of the mother or father. Therefore, the state has the power to separate those children from parents who fail to provide such an environment.

| "Even when blood relationships are strained, parents retain a vital interest in preventing the irretrievable destruction of their family life."

A State Must Produce Sufficient Evidence to Prove Parental Neglect Before Revoking Custody

The US Supreme Court's Decision

Harry Blackmun

Following evidence of parental neglect, New York State's Ulster County Department of Social Services removed John and Annie Santosky's three children from their home. The parents sued the state, arguing that the preponderance of evidence standard used to justify their children's removal was not sufficient to show the children's lives were at risk in their parents' home. When the case was finally heard by the US Supreme Court, Justice Harry Blackmun argued that when a state seeks to separate children from their biological parents permanently, the evidence against the parents must meet a higher level of scrutiny than that which was employed by the New York State Social Services. The court determined that a

Harry Blackmun, *Santosky v. Kramer*, US Supreme Court, March 24, 1982.

state must produce "clear and convincing evidence," before irrevocably severing the relationship between a child from his or her biological parents. Blackmun served as an associate justice for the US Supreme Court from 1970 until 1994.

Under New York law, the State may terminate, over parental objection, the rights of parents in their natural child upon a finding that the child is "permanently neglected." The New York Family Court Act § 622 requires that only a "fair preponderance of the evidence" support that finding. Thus, in New York, the factual certainty required to extinguish the parent-child relationship is no greater than that necessary to award money damages in an ordinary civil action.

Today we hold that the Due Process Clause of the Fourteenth Amendment demands more than this. Before a State may sever completely and irrevocably the rights of parents in their natural child, due process requires that the State support its allegations by at least clear and convincing evidence.

Little Proof Determines Neglect in New York

New York authorizes its officials to remove a child temporarily from his or her home if the child appears "neglected," within the meaning of Art. 10 of the Family Court Act. Once removed, a child under the age of 18 customarily is placed "in the care of an authorized agency," usually a state institution or a foster home. At that point, "the state's first obligation is to help the family with services to . . . reunite it. . . . But if convinced that "positive, nurturing parent-child relationships no longer exist," the State may initiate "permanent neglect" proceedings to free the child for adoption.

The State bifurcates its permanent neglect proceeding into "factfinding" and "dispositional" hearings. At the factfinding stage, the State must prove that the child has been "permanently neglected," as defined by Fam.Ct.Act §§ 614.1.(a)-(d) and Soc.Serv. Law § 384-b.7.(a). The Family Court judge then determines at a

The US Supreme Court ruled in Santosky v. Kramer *(1982) that the state must produce "clear and convincing evidence" of child neglect or endangerment before severing parental custody.* © Tina Stallard/Getty Images.

subsequent dispositional hearing what placement would serve the child's best interests.

At the factfinding hearing, the State must establish, among other things, that, for more than a year after the child entered state custody, the agency "made diligent efforts to encourage and strengthen the parental relationship." The State must further prove that, during that same period, the child's natural parents failed

> substantially and continuously or repeatedly to maintain contact with or plan for the future of the child although physically and financially able to do so.

Should the State support its allegations by "a fair preponderance of the evidence," the child may be declared permanently neglected. That declaration empowers the Family Court judge to terminate permanently the natural parents' rights in the child. Termination denies the natural parents physical custody, as well as the rights ever to visit, communicate with, or regain custody of, the child.

New York's permanent neglect statute provides natural parents with certain procedural protections. But New York permits its officials to establish "permanent neglect" with less proof than most States require. Thirty-five States, the District of Columbia, and the Virgin Islands currently specify a higher standard of proof, in parental rights termination proceedings, than a "fair preponderance of the evidence." The only analogous federal statute of which we are aware permits termination of parental rights solely upon "evidence beyond a reasonable doubt." Indian Child Welfare Act of 1978. . . . The question here is whether New York's "fair preponderance of the evidence" standard is constitutionally sufficient. . . .

Parental Choice Is Protected by the Fourteenth Amendment

Last Term, in *Lassiter v. Department of Social Services*, (1981), this Court, by a 5-4 vote, held that the Fourteenth Amendment's Due Process Clause does not require the appointment of counsel for indigent parents in every parental status termination proceeding. The case casts light, however, on the two central questions here—whether process is constitutionally due a natural parent at a State's parental rights termination proceeding, and, if so, what process is due.

In *Lassiter,* it was

> not disputed that state intervention to terminate the relationship between [a parent] and [the] child must be accomplished by procedures meeting the requisites of the Due Process Clause.

The absence of dispute reflected this Court's historical recognition that freedom of personal choice in matters of family life is a fundamental liberty interest protected by the Fourteenth Amendment.

The fundamental liberty interest of natural parents in the care, custody, and management of their child does not evaporate simply because they have not been model parents or have lost temporary custody of their child to the State. Even when blood relationships are strained, parents retain a vital interest in preventing the irretrievable destruction of their family life. If anything, persons faced with forced dissolution of their parental rights have a more critical need for procedural protections than do those resisting state intervention into ongoing family affairs. When the State moves to destroy weakened familial bonds, it must provide the parents with fundamentally fair procedures.

In *Lassiter,* the Court and three dissenters agreed that the nature of the process due in parental rights termination proceedings turns on a balancing of the "three distinct factors" specified in *Mathews v. Eldridge,* (1976): the private interests affected by the proceeding; the risk of error created by the State's chosen procedure; and the countervailing governmental interest supporting use of the challenged procedure. While the respective *Lassiter* opinions disputed whether those factors should be weighed against a presumption disfavoring appointed counsel for one not threatened with loss of physical liberty, that concern is irrelevant here. Unlike the Court's right-to-counsel rulings, its decisions concerning constitutional burdens of proof have not turned on any presumption favoring any particular standard. To the contrary, the Court has engaged in a straightforward consideration of the factors identified in *Eldridge* to determine whether a particular standard of proof in a particular proceeding satisfies due process. . . .

In parental rights termination proceedings, the private interest affected is commanding; the risk of error from using a preponderance standard is substantial; and the countervailing governmental interest favoring that standard is comparatively slight. Evaluation of the three *Eldridge* factors compels the conclusion that use of a "fair preponderance of the evidence" standard in such proceedings is inconsistent with due process.

States Must Consider Private Interests in Custody Cases

[In its ruling on *Goldberg v. Kelly* (1970) the Supreme Court found]

The extent to which procedural due process must be afforded the recipient is influenced by the extent to which he may be "condemned to suffer grievous loss."

Whether the loss threatened by a particular type of proceeding is sufficiently grave to warrant more than average certainty on the part of the factfinder turns on both the nature of the private interest threatened and the permanency of the threatened loss.

Lassiter declared it "plain beyond the need for multiple citation" that a natural parent's "desire for, and right to, 'the companionship, care, custody, and management of his or her children'" is an interest far more precious than any property right. When the State initiates a parental rights termination proceeding, it seeks not merely to infringe that fundamental liberty interest, but to end it.

> If the State prevails, it will have worked a unique kind of deprivation. . . . A parent's interest in the accuracy and justice of the decision to terminate his or her parental status is, therefore, a commanding one.

In government-initiated proceedings to determine juvenile delinquency, *In re Winship* [1970], *supra*; civil commitment, *Addington v. Texas* [1979], *supra*; deportation, *Woodby v. INS* [1966], *supra;* and denaturalization, *Chaunt v. United States* [1960], *supra,* and *Schneiderman* v. *United States* [1943], *supra*, this Court has identified losses of individual liberty sufficiently serious to warrant imposition of an elevated burden of proof. Yet juvenile delinquency adjudications, civil commitment, deportation, and denaturalization, at least to a degree, are all reversible official actions. Once affirmed on appeal, a New York decision terminating parental rights is *final* and irrevocable. Few forms of state action are both so severe and so irreversible.

Thus, the first *Eldridge* factor—the private interest affected— weighs heavily against use of the preponderance standard at a state-initiated permanent neglect proceeding. We do not deny that the child and his foster parents are also deeply interested in the outcome of that contest. But at the factfinding stage of the New York proceeding, the focus emphatically is not on them.

Parents and Their Children Should Not Be Adversaries

The factfinding does not purport—and is not intended—to balance the child's interest in a normal family home against the parents' interest in raising the child. Nor does it purport to determine whether the natural parents or the foster parents would provide the better home. Rather, the factfinding hearing pits the State directly against the parents. The State alleges that the natural parents are at fault. The questions disputed and decided are what the State did—"made diligent efforts,"—and what the natural parents did not do—"maintain contact with or plan for the future of the child." The State marshals an array of public resources to prove its case and disprove the parents' case. Victory by the State not only makes termination of parental rights possible; it entails a judicial determination that the parents are unfit to raise their own children.

At the factfinding, the State cannot presume that a child and his parents are adversaries. After the State has established parental unfitness at that initial proceeding, the court may assume at the *dispositional stage* that the interests of the child and the natural parents do diverge. But until the State proves parental unfitness, the child and his parents share a vital interest in preventing erroneous termination of their natural relationship. Thus, at the factfinding, the interests of the child and his natural parents coincide to favor use of error-reducing procedures. . . .

A Higher Standard of Evidence Would Reduce the Risk of Error

Under *Mathews v. Eldridge,* we next must consider both the risk of erroneous deprivation of private interests resulting from use of a "fair preponderance" standard and the likelihood that a higher evidentiary standard would reduce that risk. Since the

Parents' Rights in a State of Transition

On a jurisprudential level, *Santosky* [*v. Kramer*] might simply have been a compromise, middle-of-the-road decision like *Lassiter* [*v. Department of Social Services*]. In *Lassiter*, the court had a choice between not requiring and requiring counsel for indigent parents. The Court avoided either extreme and chose a moderate case-by-case approach. *Santosky* follows this trend nicely. Given the choice of three standards, the Court chose the middle ground. In both cases, the Court scrupulously avoided equating termination proceedings with either "extreme" criminal trial or civil case. In adopting this moderate position, the Court might be saying that the liberty interest of a parent in his or her offspring is one of substantial importance and worthy of protection, but not as substantial as the loss of physical liberty. . . .

Given the relative recency of the status of family rights as fundamental, the Court might actually be heading in the direction of elevating these rights to the status accorded physical liberty, but is presently in a state of transition.

Patricia J. Falk, "Why Not Beyond a Reasonable Doubt?," Nebraska Law Review, *1983.*

factfinding phase of a permanent neglect proceeding is an adversary contest between the State and the natural parents, the relevant question is whether a preponderance standard fairly allocates the risk of an erroneous factfinding between these two parties.

In New York, the factfinding stage of a state-initiated permanent neglect proceeding bears many of the indicia of a criminal trial. The Commissioner of Social Services charges the parents with permanent neglect. They are served by summons. The factfinding hearing is conducted pursuant to formal rules of evidence. The State, the parents, and the child are all represented by counsel. The State seeks to establish a series of historical facts about the intensity of its agency's efforts to reunite the family, the infrequency and insubstantiality of the parents' contacts with their child, and the parents' inability or unwillingness to formulate a plan for the child's future. The attorneys submit documentary evidence, and call witnesses who are subject to cross-examination. Based on all the evidence, the judge then determines whether the State has proved the statutory elements of permanent neglect by a fair preponderance of the evidence.

At such a proceeding, numerous factors combine to magnify the risk of erroneous factfinding. Permanent neglect proceedings employ imprecise substantive standards that leave determinations unusually open to the subjective values of the judge. In appraising the nature and quality of a complex series of encounters among the agency, the parents, and the child, the court possesses unusual discretion to underweigh probative facts that might favor the parent. Because parents subject to termination proceedings are often poor, uneducated, or members of minority groups, such proceedings are often vulnerable to judgments based on cultural or class bias.

The State Has Many Advantages in Custody Hearings

The State's ability to assemble its case almost inevitably dwarfs the parents' ability to mount a defense. No predetermined limits restrict the sums an agency may spend in prosecuting a given termination proceeding. The State's attorney usually will be expert on the issues contested and the procedures employed at the factfinding hearing, and enjoys full access to all public records concerning the family. The State may call on experts in family relations, psychology, and medicine to bolster its case. Furthermore, the primary witnesses at the hearing will be the agency's own professional caseworkers, whom the State has empowered both to investigate the family situation and to testify against the parents. Indeed, because the child is already in agency custody, the State even has the power to shape the historical events that form the basis for termination.

The disparity between the adversaries' litigation resources is matched by a striking asymmetry in their litigation options. Unlike criminal defendants, natural parents have no "double jeopardy" defense against repeated state termination efforts. If the State initially fails to win termination, as New York did here, it always can try once again to cut off the parents' rights after gathering more or better evidence. Yet even when the parents have attained the level of fitness required by the State, they have no similar means by which they can forestall future termination efforts.

Coupled with a "fair preponderance of the evidence" standard, these factors create a significant prospect of erroneous termination. A standard of proof that, by its very terms, demands consideration of the quantity, rather than the quality, of the evidence may misdirect the factfinder in the marginal case. Given the weight of the private interests at stake, the social cost of even occasional error is sizable. . . .

The Appellate Division approved New York's preponderance standard on the ground that it properly "balanced rights possessed by the child . . . with those of the natural parents. . . ." By so saying, the court suggested that a preponderance standard properly allocates the risk of error between the parents and the child. That view is fundamentally mistaken.

The court's theory assumes that termination of the natural parents' rights invariably will benefit the child. Yet we have noted above that the parents and the child share an interest in avoiding erroneous termination. Even accepting the court's assumption, we cannot agree with its conclusion that a preponderance standard fairly distributes the risk of error between parent and child. Use of that standard reflects the judgment that society is nearly neutral between erroneous termination of parental rights and erroneous failure to terminate those rights. For the child, the likely consequence of an erroneous failure to terminate is preservation of an uneasy *status quo*. For the natural parents, however, the consequence of an erroneous termination is the unnecessary destruction of their natural family. A standard that allocates the risk of error nearly equally between those two outcomes does not reflect properly their relative severity. . . .

Parents Should Not Share the Same Risk as the State in Custody Hearings

The logical conclusion of this balancing process is that the "fair preponderance of the evidence" standard prescribed by Fam. Ct.Act § 622 violates the Due Process Clause of the Fourteenth Amendment. The Court noted in *Addington:*

> The individual should not be asked to share equally with society the risk of error when the possible injury to the individual is significantly greater than any possible harm to the state.

Thus, at a parental rights termination proceeding, a near-equal allocation of risk between the parents and the State is constitutionally intolerable. . . .

A majority of the States have concluded that a "clear and convincing evidence" standard of proof strikes a fair balance between the rights of the natural parents and the State's legitimate concerns. We hold that such a standard adequately conveys to the factfinder the level of subjective certainty about his factual conclusions necessary to satisfy due process. We further hold that determination of the precise burden equal to or greater than that standard is a matter of state law properly left to state legislatures and state courts.

> "Alvin's right to a permanent, safe, and
> stable home must prevail over Lela's
> desire to continue her efforts toward
> possibly achieving adequate parenting
> and reunification."

The Safety of a Teen Parent's Child Outweighs That Parent's Right to Raise the Child

The New Jersey Superior Court's Decision

Carmen Messano

In the following ruling by the New Jersey Superior Court, Judge Carmen Messano finds that the rights of a child to experience a stable, safe, and nurturing environment in which to grow up must be privileged over the rights of his teen mother, who has not been able to provide this type of environment for him consistently. Messano carefully considers the four prongs used to determine when a parent-child relationship should be severed and concludes that in this case, the teen mother is unable to satisfy any of the conditions necessary to maintain a relationship with her son. He maintains that the state must consider whether the child will suffer from instability if a final decision regarding guardianship is continually

Carmen Messano, *New Jersey Division of Youth and Family Services v. L.J.D.*, New Jersey Superior Court, October 17, 2012.

denied. Thus, Messano finds that the parental ties between the young mother and her son will be permanently dissolved. Messano has been a superior court judge in New Jersey since August 1997.

We examine a young mother's challenges to a judgment of guardianship terminating her parental rights. Defendant L.J.D. (whom we refer to as "Lela") was fourteen when her son, A.T.D. (whom we refer to as "Alvin") was born. At that time, Lela herself was a child, who was placed in the custody and care of plaintiff, the Division of Youth and Family Services, now known as the Division of Child Protection and Permanency (the Division). As a result of Lela's custodial status, the Division assumed custody of Alvin at birth. After extending services to Lela over the ensuing years, the Division concluded she was not able to provide safe and stable care for Alvin. Consequently, the Division filed a complaint seeking guardianship and the termination of parental rights for the purpose of consenting to Alvin's adoption. Lela appeals from the judgment entered on June 27, 2011, challenging the trial judge's findings underpinning his conclusion to terminate her parental rights. She principally argues she never harmed Alvin and the Division failed to make reasonable efforts to provide her available services, which would have helped correct circumstances that led to Alvin's placement with a resource family.

After reviewing the record and applicable law in light of the arguments advanced on appeal, we uphold the trial court's findings that clear and convincing credible evidence satisfied the four statutory prongs necessary for termination of a parent's rights. Accordingly, the award of guardianship predicated on those findings is legally sound and must be affirmed. . . .

States Have an Interest in Children's Lives and Well-Being

Parents have a constitutionally protected interest in raising their biological children. [The decision in *In re Adoption of a Child by W.P. and M.P.* (App. Div. 1998) found that] "The Federal and State Constitutions protect the inviolability of family unit." However, [according to *Parham v. J.R.* (1979)] the State "is not without constitutional control over parental discretion in dealing with children when their physical or mental health is jeopardized."

The New Jersey Legislature recognizes the importance of strengthening and preserving the integrity of family life. However, in the exercise of its parens patriae [a doctrine that grants states legal authority to ensure the wellbeing of children] responsibility, it acknowledges the paramount concern remains the health and safety of the child. Therefore, children must be protected from serious physical and emotional injury and the court may examine whether "'it is in the child's best interest to preserve the family unit'" or sever the parent-child relationship.

Termination of parental rights "permanently cuts off the relationship between children and their biological parents" [as stated in *In re Guardianship of J.C.* (1992)]. "Few forms of state action are both so severe and so irreversible." *Santosky v. Kramer*, (1982). . . . The best interests standard, initially formulated by the Supreme Court in *New Jersey Division of Youth and Family Services v. A.W.*, (1986), and later codified in N.J.S.A. 30:4C-15.1a, requires the State to establish each of the following prongs by clear and convincing evidence before parental rights may be severed:

(1) The child's safety, health or development has been or will continue to be endangered by the parental relationship;

(2) The parent is unwilling or unable to eliminate the harm facing the child or is unable or unwilling to provide a safe and stable home for the child and the delay of permanent placement will add to the harm. Such harm may include evidence that separating the child from his resource family [formerly referred to as "foster"] parents would cause serious and enduring emotional or psychological harm to the child;

(3) The [D]ivision has made reasonable efforts to provide services to help the parent correct the circumstances which led to the child's placement outside the home and the court has considered alternatives to termination of parental rights; and

(4) Termination of parental rights will not do more harm than good.

These four factors are neither discrete nor separate, but are interrelated and overlap. Together they are designed to create a composite picture of "what may be necessary to promote and protect the best interests of the child" [as defined in the court's ruling in *N.J. Div. of Youth & Family Servs. v. R.L.* (2007)]. Application of the four-part test is "extremely fact sensitive[,]" requiring "particularized evidence that addresses the specific circumstances of the individual case" [according to this decision].

When a child's biological parent resists termination of parental rights, the cornerstone of the inquiry becomes whether the parent can "cease causing [his or her] child harm" and become fit to assume the parental role within time to meet the child's needs. *J.C., supra.* The analysis employs "strict standards to protect the statutory and constitutional rights of the natural parents." *Ibid.* The burden rests on the State "'to demonstrate by clear and convincing evidence' that risk of 'serious and lasting [future] harm to the child' is sufficiently great as to require severance of the parental ties." *W.P. & M.P., supra.*

On appeal, Lela challenges the sufficiency of the evidence presented, arguing the Division failed to establish each of the four prongs by clear and convincing evidence. She maintains she never endangered Alvin and no enduring harm exists. Further, her efforts toward improving her circumstances reflect her willingness and ability to eliminate any perceived harm. She also disputes the finding that the Division fulfilled its obligation to provide services, citing its refusal to secure a second "Mommy & Me" placement. Finally she rejects the proposition that severing

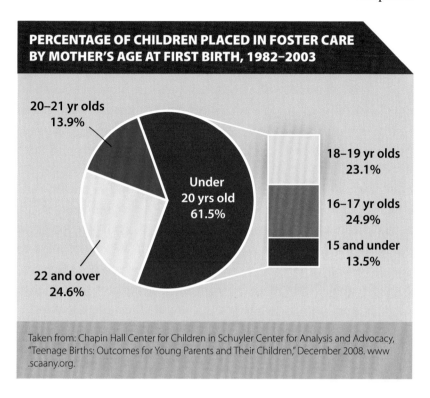

PERCENTAGE OF CHILDREN PLACED IN FOSTER CARE BY MOTHER'S AGE AT FIRST BIRTH, 1982–2003

20–21 yr olds
13.9%

Under 20 yrs old
61.5%

22 and over
24.6%

18–19 yr olds
23.1%

16–17 yr olds
24.9%

15 and under
13.5%

Taken from: Chapin Hall Center for Children in Schuyler Center for Analysis and Advocacy, "Teenage Births: Outcomes for Young Parents and Their Children," December 2008. www.scaany.org.

her parental rights would not cause Alvin more harm than good. We examine each of these contentions.

The State Must Protect Children from a Damaging Parental Relationship

Under the first prong of the best interests standard, the Division must prove by clear and convincing evidence that "[t]he child's safety, health or development has been or will continue to be endangered by the parental relationship[.]" N.J.S.A. 30:4C-15.1a(l). "[As stated in the decision for *In re Guardianship of K.H.O.* (1999)]. . . . The harm shown must be one that threatens the child's health and will likely have continuing deleterious effects on the child."

The trauma fourteen-year-old Lela suffered at the hands of her parents was discovered at the time she bore Alvin. The psychological and psychiatric assessments from 2007 and 2008 vividly depict a young teen who understandably displayed sexualized behaviors, aggressive confrontational lashing out, immaturity, and impulsivity. She needed to unwind her own emotional needs, including the conflict regarding her mother who failed to protect her from harm, as well as struggle to discern appropriate societal behaviors in the absence of role models and family support. Clearly, structure and selflessness—key concepts in childrearing—were foreign. The Division devised a course to address the multitude of needs presented by Alvin and Lela.

Lela does not disagree that she was not ready to care for Alvin when he was born. Rather she maintains the Division failed to show Alvin was harmed in her care and her youth cannot adequately justify the presence of harm. We agree a parent's age alone will not define whether she can provide adequate parenting or the capacity to avoid physical or emotional harm to her child. In this matter, Lela's impulsivity, rebellion, and poor judgment compromised Alvin's safety.

Lela's impulsive, aggressive behaviors continued almost unabated for more than a year following Alvin's birth. Her confrontational defiance precluded her success in the "Mommy & Me" program; prevented her sister from continuing as a resource in rearing Alvin; and terminated her placement at the YMWCA and a therapeutic foster home. Lela disregarded her obligation to attend school, assaulted those with whom she disagreed, disobeyed her resource parents, disregarded curfews, ran away, and battled against the structure of school. To her credit, Lela did not turn to substance abuse and other illegal conduct, continued counseling and began to accept its benefits.

We reject the notion that the Division merely removed Alvin because Lela was young when she gave birth. From Alvin's birth until the Division filed for guardianship, Lela was not able or willing to comport her behavior to focus on her son's needs. Our review of the record leaves little doubt Alvin was removed because his safety would have been compromised if placed in Lela's care. . . .

Despite Lela's lack of culpability for Alvin's initial removal, the ensuing years reflected minimal change in her ability to resolve the identified safety concerns or to achieve necessary competency in parenting. The Division is not required to wait until a child actually suffers an injury to substantiate harm justifying his removal from parental custody, pursuant to N.J.S.A. 30:4C-15.1a(l). We determine the trial court's finding regarding the Division's satisfaction of this factor is clearly and convincingly supported by the evidence of record.

The State Must Give a Parent Time to Meet the Child's Needs

The second factor of the best interests standard focuses on parental unfitness and overlaps with the proofs supporting the first prong. The court considers not only "whether the parent is fit, but also whether he or she can become fit within time to assume the parental role necessary to meet the child's needs." *R.L., supra.* Under the second prong, the standard is whether it is "reasonably foreseeable" that a parent can "cease to inflict harm upon" the child and demonstrate adequate parenting that would not place the child's physical or mental health in "substantial jeopardy[.]" *A.W., supra.* . . .

In late 2009, sixteen-year-old Lela began to accept the benefit of counseling and realized she had an obligation to fulfill Alvin's needs and not just her own. Lela repeatedly expressed love for her son and began to back up her words with her conduct in an effort to achieve reunification. She refocused on school achievements, regularly attended therapy, rarely missed visitations, and completed additional parenting skills. Dr. Fite was able to eliminate psychosis or mental illness as a barrier to reunification and found Lela was learning to control her actions and develop insight regarding how her behaviors affected others.

We do not minimize these strides. Lela rose above the victimization she suffered and assumed some direction for her life. In fact, the years of effort she has expended will provide a solid

In 2012 the New Jersey Superior Court ruled that the custody of a child may be terminated when a teen mother cannot provide a safe and stable home. © Ian Shaw/The Image Bank/ Getty Images.

foundation for parenting. However, our focus must be on Alvin. The emphasis of the Federal Adoption and Safe Families Act of 1997, Pub.L. No. 105-89, has shifted from protracted efforts for reunification with a birth parent to an expeditious, permanent placement to promote the child's well-being. "Keeping the child in limbo, hoping for some long term unification plan, would be a misapplication of the law." *N.J. Div. of Youth & Family Servs. v. A.G.*, (App.Div.2001). When viewing the facts through the prism of Alvin's needs, as the law requires, the uncontroverted record reflects Lela could not grasp the nature and necessity of prioritizing Alvin's needs above her own and never achieved an appreciation for the young child's need for stability. Accordingly, Alvin remains at risk if placed in her care. . . .

We are satisfied the record supports the trial judge's conclusion that the Division has satisfied the second prong by clear and convincing evidence. The chaos of Lela's life has lessened but has not ended, with likely more uncertainty when her baby arrives. Despite the three years that have passed and the myriad of efforts extended, Lela's life remains unstable and she continues to be unable to provide Alvin a safe and stable home. Further, delay in satisfying Alvin's need for a permanent placement will add to his harm. "A child is not chattel in which a parent has an untempered property right" and should not "be held prisoner of the rights of others, even those of his or her parents." *N.J. Div. of Youth and Family Servs. v. C.S.*, (2004).

Finally, we reject Lela's contention the trial court's determination was an erroneous value judgment on the quality of her parenting versus that of the foster parents. The Division's evidence exposed the risks of harm if Alvin were placed in his mother's care, whether in a "Mommy & Me" program or not. Under these circumstances, continued reunification efforts were not justified.

Reasonable Services Must Be Provided to Assist Parents

The third prong of the best interests standard requires the Division to make "reasonable efforts to provide services to help the parent correct the circumstances" that necessitated removal and placement of the child in foster care. N.J.S.A. 30:4C-15.1a(3). "Reasonable efforts" consist of services "to assist the parents in remedying the circumstances and conditions that led to the placement of the child and in reinforcing the family structure [.]" N.J.S.A. 30:4C-15.1c.

The reasonableness of the efforts depends upon the facts and circumstances of each case. Provision of services under the third prong "contemplates efforts that focus on reunification[,]" *K.H.O., supra*, and "may include consultation with the parent, developing a plan for reunification, providing services essential to the realization of the reunification plan, informing the family of the child's progress, and facilitating visitation." *M.M., supra*. The services provided to meet the child's need for permanency and the parent's right to reunification must be "'coordinated'" and must have a "'realistic potential'" to succeed. (App.Div.2002). . . .

The one-hundred exhibits introduced by the Division at trial are replete with services extended, spanning from May 2007 through May 2011, in an effort to reunite Lela and Alvin. These services addressed medical, logistical, educational, housing, psychological, psychiatric, and financial needs along with the provision of years of visitation, one year of parenting classes, life skills, years of anger management, individual therapy, and other counseling. The Division continued its efforts to educate Lela on the obligations of care involved in being a mother, not mere rote tasks of diapering and feeding. Even in light of setbacks, services continued, aimed at Lela's individual healing as well as nurturing her son.

Following our review of the evidence, we determine the Division has met the heightened burden resulting from Lela's custodial status, the extent and nature of which accorded with her youth, and attempted to achieve reunification. We find no flaw in the trial judge's determination the Division extended reasonable efforts in this case. . . .

In the three years prior to trial, Lela unquestionably matured. Yet, contrary to her suggestion, she had not fully complied with the Division's services. Most notably, she continued to disrupt her placements in favor of relationship decisions found detrimental to Alvin's interests. In this significant regard, Lela has not achieved the level of stability and security necessary to care for a young child. She argues her conduct was reasonable in light of the Division's failure to find a new placement fast enough. Such a suggestion deflects her responsibility for her conduct and disregards the fact her choices remained motivated by fulfilling her interests, desires, and needs, without regard to the resultant impact on Alvin.

The Division's decision to pursue termination of parental rights rather than continue to hope Lela would modify her conduct was reasonably focused on Alvin's paramount need for safety, security, and permanency. Considering the totality of the circumstances, we conclude the Division's efforts to achieve reunification were reasonable. Moreover, it was not unreasonable to decline modification of Alvin's permanency plan to allow Lela another attempt in a "Mommy & Me" program, in light of evidence the effort would not have a "'realistic potential'" to succeed.

The Child's Need for Stability

Under the last prong of the best interests standard, the Division must prove the child will not suffer greater harm from the termination of ties with his biological parent than from the permanent disruption of his relationship with his resource family. The overriding consideration under this prong remains the child's need for permanency and stability. If a child can be returned to the parental home without endangering his health and safety, the parent's right to reunification takes precedence over the permanency plan. On the other hand, "termination of parental rights likely will not do more harm than good" where the child has bonded with the resource parents in a nurturing and safe home. *N.J. Div. of Youth & Family Servs. v. E.P.* (2008). The Division's clear and convincing evidence "must show 'that separating the child from his or her foster parents would cause serious and enduring emotional or psychological harm.'". . . In meeting its burden under this prong, the Division should adduce testimony from a "well qualified expert who has had full opportunity to make a comprehensive, objective, and informed evaluation" of the child's relationship with the natural and resource parents. *J.C., supra.*

Lela agrees Alvin's bond with his resource parents was stronger than his bond to her. However, she argues the trial judge erroneously disregarded the fact she too was strongly bonded to Alvin and expert recommendations provided for reunification. We disagree. . . .

While Alvin has a relationship with Lela, the harm he would face were those ties severed would not be enduring, as it would be properly mitigated by his resource parents. This result is additionally supported by the trial court's finding that further delay in establishing a stable and permanent home for Alvin, who has been in placement for almost the entirety of his life (now more than four years), would continue to cause harm. . . .

In conclusion, we determine the trial court's findings are properly supported by clear and convincing evidence and the legal conclusions drawn therefrom will not be disturbed. Alvin's right to a permanent, safe, and stable home must prevail over Lela's desire to continue her efforts toward possibly achieving adequate parenting and reunification.

> *"This minor child, the only truly innocent party, is entitled to support from both her parents regardless of their ages."*

Minor Fathers Must Make Child Support Payments for Children They Conceive

The Kansas Supreme Court's Decision

Richard Winn Holmes

The following viewpoint presents the 1993 ruling of the Kansas Supreme Court in the case Hermesmann v. Seyer. *This case sought to determine whether a male who conceived a child when he was younger than the age of consent should be held financially responsible for that child and required to make child support payments. Chief Justice Richard Winn Holmes ruled that even if a young man is legally unable to "consent" to sexual intercourse at the time he fathers a child, he is still responsible for helping to support that child financially as he or she grows. Thus, Holmes found that Seyer must make child support payments to his daughter's mother. In the ruling, Holmes cites a range of court cases from different states that came to similar conclusions about minor fathers' responsibilities to their children. Holmes served on the Kansas Supreme Court as*

Richard Winn Holmes, *Hermesmann v. Seyer*, Kansas Supreme Court, March 5, 1993.

*a judge from 1977 until 1990, when he became the chief justice, a
position that he held until his retirement in 1995.*

The facts, as best we can determine them from an inadequate
record, do not appear to be seriously in dispute.

Colleen Hermesmann routinely provided care for Shane
Seyer as a baby sitter or day care provider during 1987 and 1988.
The two began a sexual relationship at a time when Colleen was
16 years old and Shane was only 12. The relationship continued
over a period of several months and the parties engaged in sexual
intercourse on an average of a couple of times a week. As a result,
a daughter, Melanie, was born to Colleen on May 30, 1989. At
the time of the conception of the child, Shane was 13 years old
and Colleen was 17. Colleen applied for and received financial
assistance through the Aid to Families with Dependent Children
program (ADC) from [the Kansas Department of Social and
Rehabilitation Services] SRS. . . .

On March 8, 1991, SRS filed a petition on behalf of Colleen
Hermesmann, alleging that Shane Seyer was the father of
Colleen's minor daughter, Melanie. The petition also alleged
that SRS had provided benefits through the ADC program to
Colleen on behalf of the child and that Colleen had assigned
support rights due herself and her child to SRS. The petition re-
quested that the court determine paternity and order Shane to
reimburse SRS for all assistance expended by SRS on Melanie's
behalf. On December 17, 1991, an administrative hearing officer
found Shane was Melanie's biological father. The hearing officer
further determined that Shane was not required to pay the birth
expenses or any of the child support expenses up to the date of
the hearing on December 17, 1991, but that Shane had a duty to
support the child from the date of the hearing forward. . . .

The court found that the issue of Shane's consent was irrel-
evant and ordered Shane to pay child support of $50 per month.
The court also granted SRS a joint and several judgment against
Shane and Colleen in the amount of $7,068, for assistance

provided by the ADC program on behalf of Melanie through February 1992. The judgment included medical and other birthing expenses as well as assistance paid after Melanie's birth. Shane appeals the judgment rendered and the order for continuing support but does not contest the trial court's paternity finding. . . .

Paternal Responsibility Does Not Change Based on Age

Shane asserts as his first issue that, because he was a minor under the age of 16 at the time of conception, he was legally incapable of consenting to sexual intercourse and therefore cannot be held legally responsible for the birth of his child. Shane cites no case law to directly support this proposition. Instead, he argues that Colleen Hermesmann sexually assaulted him, that he was the victim of the crime of statutory rape, and that the criminal statute of indecent liberties with a child should be applied to hold him incapable of consenting to the act. . . .

Although the issue of whether an underage alleged "victim" of a sex crime can be held liable for support of a child born as a result of such crime is one of first impression in Kansas, other jurisdictions have addressed the question.

In *In re Paternity of J.L.H.*, (1989), J.J.G. appealed from a summary judgment in a paternity proceeding determining that he was the father of J.L.H. and ordering him to pay child support equal to 17 percent of his gross income. J.J.G. was 15 years old when the child was conceived. On appeal, he asserted that the child's mother, L.H., sexually assaulted him, contrary to Wis. Stat. 940.225(2)(e) (1979) (the Wisconsin statutory rape statute in effect at the time), and that, as a minor, he was incapable of consent under the sexual assault law. The court rejected this argument and stated . . . :

> We reject appellant's assertion that because he was fifteen years old when he had intercourse with L.H., he was incapable of consent. The assertion rests on the argument that sec. 940.225(4)

In Hermesmann v. Seyer *(1993), the Kansas Supreme Court ruled that minor fathers can be required to provide financial support for a child they conceive.* © iStockphoto.com/Justin Horrocks.

(a), Stats. 1979, created a rebuttable presumption to that effect. That statute pertains to the guilt of a criminal defendant, not to the civil rights or duties of the victim. Paternity actions are civil proceedings. The presumption created by sec. 940.225(4) (a) does not apply in this proceeding. 149 Wis.2d at 355–57.

The court then goes on to state: "If voluntary intercourse results in parenthood, then for purposes of child support, the parenthood is voluntary. This is true even if a fifteen-year old boy's parenthood resulted from a sexual assault upon him within the meaning of the criminal law."

Although the question of whether the intercourse with Colleen was "voluntary," as the term is usually understood, is not specifically before us, it was brought out in oral argument before this court that the sexual relationship between Shane and his baby sitter, Colleen, started when he was only 12 years old and lasted over a period of several months. At no time did Shane register any complaint to his parents about the sexual liaison with Colleen.

In *Schierenbeck v. Minor*, (1961), Schierenbeck, a 16-year-old boy, appealed the adjudication in a dependency proceeding that he was the father of a child born to a 20-year-old woman. On appeal, Schierenbeck cited a Colorado criminal statute which defined rape in the third degree by a female of a male person under the age of 18 years. In discussing the relevance of the criminal statute, the court stated:

> Certain it is that [Schierenbeck's] assent to the illicit act does not exclude commission of the statutory crime, but it has nothing to do with assent as relating to progeny. His youth is basic to the crime; it is not a factor in the question of whether he is the father of [the child].
>
> 'The putative father may be liable in bastardy proceedings for the support and maintenance of his child, even though he is a minor. . . .' Bastards, 10 C.J.S. 152, 53. If Schierenbeck is adjudged to be the father of [the child] after a proper hearing

and upon sufficient evidence, he should support [the child] under this fundamental doctrine. 148 Colo. at 586.

The trial court decision was reversed on other grounds not pertinent to the facts of our case and remanded for further proceedings.

Minor Parents Must Support Their Children

The Kansas Parentage Act, K.S.A. 38-1110 et seq., specifically contemplates minors as fathers and makes no exception for minor parents regarding their duty to support and educate their child. K.S.A. 38-1117 provides, in part:

> If a man alleged or presumed to be the father is a minor, the court shall cause notice of the pendency of the proceedings and copies of the pleadings on file to be served upon the parents or guardian of the minor and shall appoint a guardian ad litem [a party appointed by a court to act in a lawsuit on behalf of another party] who shall be an attorney to represent the minor in the proceedings.

K.S.A. 1992 Supp. 38-1121(c) provides, in part:

> Upon adjudging that a party is the parent of a minor child, the court shall make provision for support and education of the child including the necessary medical expenses incident to the birth of the child. The court may order the support and education expenses to be paid by either or both parents for the minor child.

If the legislature had wanted to exclude minor parents from responsibility for support, it could easily have done so.

As previously stated, Shane does not contest that he is the biological father of the child. As a father, he has a common-law duty, as well as a statutory duty, to support his minor child. This duty applies equally to parents of children born out of wedlock.

National Policy on Teen Fathers' Child Support Enforcement Is Lacking

The treatment of teenage fathers by the CSE [Child Support Enforcement] program is not well understood at a national level. While there is greater uniformity in the amount of child support ordered within states, across-state variation is the norm. With regards to the establishment of paternity and support orders and the enforcement of child support for teen fathers, within-state uniformity is the exception. State and local jurisdictions are denied the benefit of a well-articulated national policy on the treatment of teenage fathers. This lack of direction undoubtedly stems in large part from our lack of information concerning the characteristics of the teenage father population.

Maureen A. Pirog-Good and David H. Good,
"Child Support Enforcement for Teen Fathers'
Problems and Prospects," Institute for Research
on Poverty Discussion Paper No. 1029–94,
February 1994.

Under the statutory and common law of this state, Shane owes a duty to support his minor child. K.S.A. 1992 Supp. 21-3503 does not apply to a civil proceeding and cannot serve to relieve Shane of his legal responsibilities towards his child. Shane relies upon six cases to support his position: *State v. Fike*, (1988); *State v. Hutchcraft*, (1987); *State v. Lilley*, (1982); *State v. Price*, (1974); *State v. Eberline*, (1891); *State v. Fulcher*, (1987). Each of these cases involves the age of consent issue under the Kansas statutory rape law and its present equivalent. We conclude that the issue of consent to sexual activity under the criminal statutes is irrelevant in a civil action to determine paternity and for support of the minor child of such activity.

Consequently, Shane's reliance on the foregoing criminal cases is misplaced.

The Minor Child's Rights Must Be Protected

For Shane's next issue, he asserts that it is not sound public policy for a court to order a youth to pay child support for a child conceived during the crime of indecent liberties with a child when the victim was unable to consent to the sexual intercourse. He claims that while the Kansas Parentage Act creates a State interest in the welfare of dependent relatives, the policy behind the Parentage Act is not to force a minor, who is unable to consent to sexual intercourse, to support a child born from the criminal act.

Shane provides no case law specifically on point, but once again relies upon the Kansas cases involving statutory rape. He also refers the court to K.S.A. 39-718a, which authorized the Secretary of SRS to collect child support from an absent parent. Shane suggests that underlying K.S.A. 39-718a is the presumption that a parent consented to the conception, and argues that the proper remedy for SRS in this case is to seek support exclusively from Colleen Hermesmann, as she was the only parent legally able to consent to the conception of the child. What Shane has failed to recognize, however, is that K.S.A. 39-718a was repealed by the legislature in 1988. Any argument based upon a statute which was repealed five years ago is obviously without merit.

However, the argument of two allegedly conflicting public policies of this state does merit consideration. Other jurisdictions have recognized the conflict between a State's interest in protecting juveniles and a State's interest in requiring parental support of children. In *In re Parentage of J.S.*, (1990), the trial court ordered a minor father to pay child support for his illegitimate son. The minor father appealed the order, but did not contest the trial court's paternity finding. In affirming the trial court's decision ordering support, the court stated:

The respondent initially argues that he should not be required to support his child, because he was a 15-year-old minor when the child was conceived. He contends that Illinois public policy protects minors from the consequences of their improvident conduct.

We note that contrary to the respondent's position, Illinois public policy has never offered blanket protection to reckless minors. [Citations omitted.] At the same time, Illinois public policy has recognized the blanket right of every child to the physical, mental, emotional, and monetary support of his or her parents. The public has an interest in protecting children from becoming wards of the State.

In the instant case, we find that the public policy mandating parental support of children overrides any policy of protecting a minor from improvident acts. We therefore hold that the trial court properly found that the respondent was financially responsible for his child. (Emphasis added.)

In *Commonwealth v. A Juvenile*, (1982), a 16-year-old father was ordered to pay child support of $8 a week toward the support of his child born out of wedlock. The minor father admitted his paternity, but appealed the support order. On appeal, the court affirmed the judgment of the lower court and said:

The defendant's claim rests on an assertion that a support order is inconsistent with the statutory purpose of treating a juvenile defendant as a child 'in need of aid, encouragement and guidance.' [Citation omitted.] Although we acknowledge that purpose, we see no basis, and certainly no statutory basis, for concluding that a juvenile should be free from any duty to support his or her illegitimate child. The illegitimate child has interests, as does the Commonwealth.

This State's interest in requiring minor parents to support their children overrides the State's competing interest in protecting juveniles from improvident acts, even when such acts may include criminal activity on the part of the other parent.

Considering the three persons directly involved, Shane, Colleen, and Melanie, the interests of Melanie are superior, as a matter of public policy, to those of either or both of her parents. This minor child, the only truly innocent party, is entitled to support from both her parents regardless of their ages.

| "Adolescent fathers must be recognized and respected, not just for the financial support they may be able to provide, but for the psychological and emotional support they can provide."

Economic Support and the Dilemma of Teen Fathers

Judith Rozie-Battle

In the following viewpoint, Judith Rozie-Battle argues that while much attention has been paid to the rise in teen pregnancy in recent decades, policymakers must readjust their focus to include teen fathers and their role in raising their children. Battle maintains that this lack of concentration on teen fathers has resulted from a general de-emphasis on the role of fathers. Instead of encouraging fathers to initiate and foster a growing relationship with their children, she states that current policies only require financial support, something that can be difficult for teen fathers to provide. Battle calls for a reevaluation of current child support and paternity policy, especially with regard to teen fathers, and promotes easy to understand, inclusive policy that allows young fathers to be active participants in their children's lives. Rozie-Battle is a former social welfare policy professor and currently serves as a senior program officer at the Hartford Foundation for Public Giving.

Judith Rozie-Battle, "Economic Support and the Dilemma of Teen Fathers," *Journal of Health and Social Policy*, vol. 17, no. 1, 2003. Reprinted by permission of the publisher (Taylor and Francis Ltd. www.tandf.co.uk/journals).

Young, unmarried fathers are rarely the focus in child support enforcement literature. A few articles discuss low-income fathers, or absent fathers, but they rarely discuss the consequences of child support enforcement efforts for adolescent fathers. The child support policies of this nation apply to these young men— as they do to all parents. Yet, there are special considerations that must be addressed for adolescent fathers.

The Role of Fathers

The role of the father has been subjugated in America. Society has traditionally delegated the psychological and developmental needs of the child as a responsibility and obligation of the mother. Societal attitudes toward adolescent fathers are no different than the attitudes toward fathers in general. This role has been reinforced over the years in many circumstances, including the legal presumption referred to as the "tender years doctrine." This doctrine dates back to the late 1800s and early 1900s when fathers were still generally awarded custody of their children following divorce. In an effort to counter this one-sided practice, this doctrine was developed to take the needs of the children into consideration. It made the assumption that the well-being of children, particularly young children under the age of seven, would be better served by being placed with their mothers in any custody disputes. Although this doctrine has been abolished in almost every jurisdiction, the actions of individual judges and courts indicate it is still a common practice.

Traditionally the father has not been viewed as a parent, instead he has been perceived as a spouse/partner for the mother of the child and as a financial resource. "[E]xcept for his financial contribution, the father is a disposable parent" [stated religion professor Jerry W. McCant]. In the case of young fathers, the financial contribution is usually lacking or so minuscule that he indeed is a disposable parent in the eyes of society. The psychological message we send to young men is that the father is the perpetrator and the mother the victim.

This description has changed very little over the past twenty years. Despite changes in family compositions, between 1950 and 1994 the percentage of children living in mother-only families climbed from six percent to 24 percent. In recent years there has been an increase in the number of fathers who choose to stay home and raise their children while the spouse/mother pursues her career. Despite this increase, the number of fathers involved with their children and sharing in the day-to-day rearing of their children are still the minority. The role of fathers continues to be defined generally in terms of financial contributions. This is particularly true for fathers of children receiving public support as evidenced by the increased national child support enforcement efforts.

In his study of divorced fathers, [social work professor Edward] Kruk found fathers disengage from their children soon after separation and that over time that disengagement increases. These fathers identified the loss of the father/child relationship as one of the most salient factors in their transition. Those fathers who were close to their children felt more loss, while others found new ways to relate to their children and in fact adapted to the new role of part-time visiting dad. Data from the National Commission on Children and other research supports the fact those fathers who do not live with their children lose contact with them over time. There is no reason to believe it would or should be any different for adolescent fathers. Fathers need to be nurtured in order to build healthy relationships with their families. When the father is connected with his child, emotional bonds are created and the home environment is positively affected. For the sake of our children and the future, fathers must be seen as more than just financial providers.

There is a belief that a father who pays child support will desire to be involved with his children. The potential for increased involvement of fathers with their children may be an upside to the strict child support enforcement efforts. However, it would be fallacy to assume that every father who pays child support will automatically desire to spend more quality time with his children. Furthermore, in some circumstances it may be necessary to be cautious about fathers having contact with their children, because it may not be in the best interest of the child. For example, in families where issues of violence or poor role modeling are present or are a major concern, safeguards must be put in place for the safety and well-being of the children. However, these situations should not be considered the norm and should not preclude encouraging fathers to be involved with their children. The bottom line is that in most situations, it is better for children to know and have contact with their fathers.

The political environment in America today has swung toward less public assistance and more personal responsibility. This "mood" has allowed policy makers to introduce and implement legislation that increases efforts to collect child support payments from absent parents to support their children. Since fathers are overwhelmingly the absent parent, the psychological message sent to fathers is clear—pay or no contact. . . .

Adolescent Fathers

An adolescent male who becomes a father is expected to embody the father role while he is still negotiating the developmental tasks of adolescence. Depending upon his own cognitive and psychosocial development, he may or may not be able to provide emotional support for a young mother and contribute to the nurturance of their offspring.

In addition, several prejudicial social factors, including the economic and social welfare systems, exclude adolescent fathers from continuing the relationship with their partners and actively participating in their children's upbringing. Often the adolescent father is unmarried and physically separated at the time of the child's birth and early childhood, thereby reducing the number of opportunities available for interaction with the infant. These young men often encounter rejection and anger from the mother

Some believe that the emotional support of teen fathers should be just as important an issue as financial support in child support cases. © Hans Neleman/Taxi/Getty Images.

of the child, resulting in limited contact with the child. They may also fear they are unable to provide financial support and may face rejection from other family members. A teen father's absence leads to a common misconception of noncaring among health care providers who often perceive adolescent fathers as irresponsible deserters of their children. The divorce rate for adolescent parents is five times higher than for adults. The unrealistic expectations of adolescent mothers about the father's marriage plans, coupled with the reality that most adolescent fathers are not interested in marriage, may further contribute to the negative view of the adolescent father so prevalent in the literature. In fact, many young fathers believe they are not prepared for fatherhood and have difficulty assuming the responsibilities at this stage of their development. . . .

Young Fathers—A Special Case

There is a disconnection between what young fathers think they know and what they actually know. Adolescent fathers lack a clear understanding of the child support enforcement laws and the applicability of these laws to them.

Young men need to realize that fatherhood during adolescence makes them subject to support obligations until the child is at least eighteen years of age. Child support enforcement efforts have been strengthened over the past ten years and many young men believe that because in prior years they were not required to provide support, they will not be required to do so in the future. They also believe that if they are unemployed they will not be held accountable for child support payments. Finally, they do not understand that if they do not pay child support from the time the child is born, they can be held responsible for past payments. This will occur when they obtain a job or acquire a better paying job in the future. These young men must be made aware of the laws that are designed to ensure that children are supported by both parents.

Much of the child support enforcement effort focuses on withholding income from fathers to support their children. For many young fathers this is difficult because of age or skill levels. Based on statistics from 1999, the U.S. Labor Department, unemployment rates for young white men between the ages of 16 and 21 were 13%, while African American men of the same age range experienced an unemployment rate of 31%. Consequently, many young fathers are able to pay little, if anything at all, toward child support. As Jeff Johnson of the National Center for Strategic Non-Profit Planning and Community Leadership in Washington, DC, has said, "these dads are dead broke, not dead beat."

Young fathers have the option of having a judgment reserved or a minimal order put in place, while they are still in school and unemployed or able to work only part-time. Unfortunately, many young men are not aware of this option and consequently do not take advantage of it. This option does not free the young father from supporting his children, but does allow him to make a reasonable effort, with the understanding that as his income increases, the order will be adjusted accordingly.

Some states have not enforced delinquent child support payments on minor fathers, while others, such as Texas, have prosecuted minor fathers for failure to pay child support. Other states have taken a stronger position and enacted "grandparent liability" statutes to ensure financial support for children born to teen fathers. Wisconsin, for example, has a statute that provides that if a young man is under the age of eighteen and in school, the court may order his parents to help with the support of their grandchild. This statute is an example of the policies that many young men and their parents are commonly not aware of or do not fully understand the ramifications. It is important to note the application of this law is uneven, resulting in inconsistent enforcement. Finally, some states have developed community services obligations for minor fathers in lieu of child support.

Information regarding paternity and child support enforcement efforts are critical for young men to assist them in making decisions regarding sexual activity and potential fatherhood. The families of these young men, the churches, schools, and community social service organizations that work with young parents must include fathers and provide them with the knowledge to help them make informed and responsible decisions. Prevention programs that reach young men prior to their becoming fathers are most critical. Educational and support programs that begin early and are honest, factual, and straightforward are most likely to benefit young men.

Implications for Practitioners and Policymakers

Although there has been an increase in the number of programs that serve adolescent fathers, the numbers remain relatively small. Some programs claim to work with "young parents," but

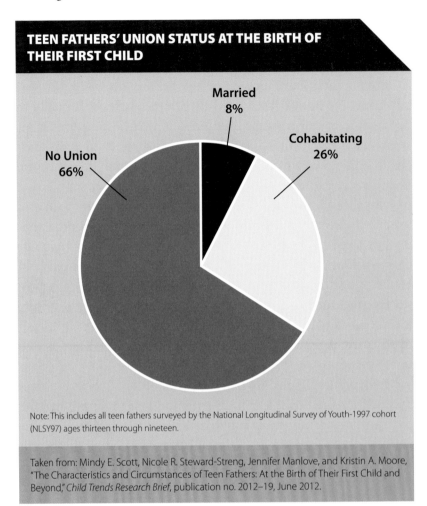

TEEN FATHERS' UNION STATUS AT THE BIRTH OF THEIR FIRST CHILD

Married
8%

Cohabitating
26%

No Union
66%

Note: This includes all teen fathers surveyed by the National Longitudinal Survey of Youth-1997 cohort (NLSY97) ages thirteen through nineteen.

Taken from: Mindy E. Scott, Nicole R. Steward-Streng, Jennifer Manlove, and Kristin A. Moore, "The Characteristics and Circumstances of Teen Fathers: At the Birth of Their First Child and Beyond," *Child Trends Research Brief*, publication no. 2012–19, June 2012.

when looking at their goals, objectives, and services, they are clearly focused on the young mother and/or the child. The focus of many adolescent parenting programs is twofold: primary prevention and support services. Unfortunately most programs continue to focus their efforts on the young mother. Prevention programs can be further divided into primary and secondary prevention services. Primary prevention services are those programs designed to prevent first pregnancies and secondary prevention services focus on the prevention of subsequent pregnancies. Both types of prevention programs are critical for young fathers. We must address the prevention of initial pregnancies and the issue of subsequent pregnancies with young men as well as young women.

Many fathers provide for their children through methods other than formal cash support payments. The "Pamper defense" is one that refers to the type of support many young fathers feel is acceptable and attainable for them. When asked whether they support their children, many young fathers say, "Yes, I buy Pampers and clothes." Yet our system has not developed a means of taking these types of contributions into account. . . . The Internal Revenue Service provides for and allows non-profit organizations to count and credit organizations and individuals for in-kind contributions, but we have yet to figure out how to do this for young fathers, and in many cases, poor fathers. This is not to say that these non-cash contributions are sufficient or the only contributions needed to raise a child, but they may be the only contributions these young men can realistically provide at this point in their lives.

Policy makers and program directors need to work toward policies that look at the true potential of fathers. This is particularly true in the poorer and culturally diverse communities in America. Examples include strengthening existing support enforcement programs to assist young fathers with job training programs and completion of high school or a GED. Services should be readily available and not restricted solely to those with TANF eligibility. Although some states are beginning to de-tangle the TANF eligibility and job training eligibility, it is neither consistent nor sufficient in practice. The utilization of community and technical colleges is also an inexpensive and focused method of obtaining concrete skills and training for young fathers.

The delivery of services needs to be revamped to focus on supportive services, including outreach and a friendly environment, as opposed to approaching the services from a "victim/ perpetrator" mentality.

There must be further development and an increase in community education programs similar to those used in HIV and substance abuse efforts. Determining what has worked in those venues could provide a model for pregnancy prevention programs for young men.

Finally, we must determine which existing programs are most effective and replicate them as much as possible. For example, outcomes-based research provides some guidance for the type of programs that are most effective. The general findings indicate that community-based clinics are more effective than school-based clinics.

As an international leader among nations, we need to better educate and inform young people, both male and female, as well as their parents/guardians of the rights and responsibilities of parenthood. They must be informed about the laws and the effect they may have on them personally. Policies must be written in plain language so that the average person affected by them can understand what is being said and how it applies to them. Parents and/or guardians must be aware of the consequences for them as the parents of adolescents who may become parents early.

We must incorporate into our youth development programming the consequences of having children early. To focus solely on the issue of abstinence limits the development of our young people and deprives them of the information they need regarding the rights, responsibilities, and consequences for early parenthood. The opportunity to make choices through informed consent is critical for the development of young men and for a successful prevention effort.

Policy makers must look at methods of encouraging payments early and regularly, even if the payments are small. Setting payments at realistic levels that fathers can attain will assist fathers in making and maintaining their payment schedules.

Policymakers further need to understand the needs of the community and the people who are affected by the decisions they make. Advisory groups of young people need to have input on the policies. This process will help develop young people into productive adults and community members who feel they have a stake in the prevention efforts. Use of peer leaders and peer counselors can also be a productive use of young people in the effort to stem early parenthood.

Child support and paternity adjudication policies need to be reviewed and made more flexible and consumer friendly. Policies and programs should encourage non-custodial fathers, particularly young fathers, to seek out services to assist them with providing financial support for their children. These programs should also provide supportive services to fathers who desire more involvement with their children.

Adolescent fathers must be recognized and respected, not just for the financial support they may be able to provide, but for the psychological and emotional support they can provide for their children. A review of current policies to determine how consistently these policies conform with the capabilities and realities of young fathers is important, particularly in light of the earning power of young men ages 16–21. Another area that needs further review is the impact present policies have on young fathers in terms of fostering relationships with their children.

Finally, policy makers and the courts must look beyond the legal issues of establishing paternity and financial support for children. Although this is certainly critical, they must also strengthen and fund community services that can assist young fathers to become more personally involved in the lives of their children.

"Regulations promulgated under
Title IX unequivocally apply its
prohibition against sex discrimination
to discrimination on the basis of
pregnancy and parental status."

A School's National Honor Society Cannot Deny Membership to a Student Parent

The US District Court's Decision

William Odis Bertelsman

In the spring of 1998, two Kentucky high school juniors, who were also mothers, were denied admittance to the Grant County High School National Honor Society (NHS). While the school's NHS chapter maintained that it had the right to consider an individual's decision to engage in premarital sex as a part of their character assessment, the girls sued on the grounds that they were discriminated against because they had become pregnant as high school students. In the following district court ruling, Judge William Odis Bertelsman finds that the Grant County NHS violated Title IX regulations that forbid discrimination on the basis of sex, pregnancy, or parental status. He found the club's actions to be discriminatory

William Odis Bertelsman, *Chipman v. Grant County School District*, US District Court, December 28, 1998.

because the only two students who were excluded from member-ship, even though they met all admission criteria, were pregnant or had given birth to a child. Thus, even if the club did not intention-ally discriminate against the girls, their actions amounted to dis-crimination and therefore must be reversed. The ruling called for the two students to be admitted to the NHS unless the court later determined that the club's rules were not in violation of Title IX regulation. Bertelsman is a US federal judge who has served since his appointment to the court in 1979.

This is a Title IX, 20 U.S.C. Sections 1681–88, action for dis-crimination in educational programs. In addition, plaintiffs allege that defendants violated their state and federal constitu-tional rights to equal protection and unduly interfered in their state and federal rights to privacy and personal autonomy. . . .

The National Honor Society of Secondary Schools (NHS) recognizes high school students for outstanding achievement. High schools may establish a local NHS chapter upon paying a chartering fee and annual initiation fee to the NHS. Chapters are required to adopt the NHS constitution, but each chapter may establish different admission criteria so long as those criteria are consistent with the NHS constitution. A pertinent provision of the NHS handbook provides:

> It should be noted that, under provisions of federal law, preg-nancy—whether within or without wedlock—cannot be the basis for automatic denial of the right to participate in any public school activity. It may properly be considered, however, like any other circumstance, as a factor to be assessed in deter-mining character as it applies to the National Honor Society. But pregnancy may be taken into account in determining character only if evidence of paternity is similarly regarded.

Grant County High School has established a local NHS chap-ter. As required by the NHS constitution, those offered admis-sion to the Grant County NHS must demonstrate outstanding

Title IX Must Be Strengthened to Protect Pregnant Students' Rights

The Regulations implementing and governing Title IX were intended to protect pregnant students from sex discrimination in school, but they are inadequate to address all of the unique challenges raised by pregnant students. The regulatory provisions governing pregnancy discrimination in schools have faded into the background, partially because their noisy neighbor, the provisions governing female participation in school athletics, have taken so much of the attention given to the Regulations. Despite numerous attempts by commentators to raise concerns about the continuing discrimination suffered by pregnant students, little has changed since the Regulations were enacted. In order to truly guarantee access, choice, and quality education to pregnant students, the Regulations must change. Stronger Regulations are the most likely vehicle to positive changes for pregnant students, which have been a long time coming and much needed to fulfill the promise of equality in Title IX.

> *Kendra Fershee, "Hollow Promises for Pregnant Students: How the Regulations Governing Title IX Fail to Prevent Pregnancy Discrimination in Schools,"* Indiana Law Review, *January 1, 2009.*

scholarship, service, leadership, and character. Although the NHS permits anyone with a grade point average of 3.0 or better to be considered for admission, the Grant County chapter requires a grade point average of at least 3.5.

Plaintiffs are both seniors at Grant County High School. Both plaintiffs have grade point averages substantially above 3.5. On April 23, 1996, Chasity Glass gave birth to a daughter. On June 1, 1998, Somer Hurston (nee Chipman) gave birth to a daughter. As early as November 1997, it was generally known around Grant County High School that Ms. Hurston was pregnant. In the Spring of 1998, when plaintiffs were juniors, the GCNHS selection committee voted to offer NHS membership to every junior with a 3.5 or better grade point average except the plaintiffs. There is strong evidence that the GCNHS selection committee considered the fact that each plaintiff had engaged in premarital sexual activity and had given birth to a child out of wedlock. There is further strong evidence that the selection committee did not ask those students offered admission to the NHS—male or female—if they had engaged in premarital sexual activity. However, the evidence before the court indicates that the committee would have considered any evidence of paternity in evaluating the character of male students, but that it was unlikely that any such knowledge would come before the committee in any way but rumor and gossip. . . .

Schools Cannot Discriminate Against Pregnant Students

Title IX prohibits sex discrimination in any educational program or activity receiving federal financial assistance. Specifically, Title IX provides in part:

> No person in the United States shall, on the basis of sex, be excluded from participation in, be denied the benefits of, or be subjected to discrimination under any education program or activity receiving Federal financial assistance. 20 U.S.C. § 1681(a).

Regulations promulgated under Title IX unequivocally apply its prohibition against sex discrimination to discrimination on the basis of pregnancy and parental status, stating:

> A recipient [of federal funds, such as Grant County Schools] shall not apply any rule concerning a student's actual or potential parental, family, or marital status which treats students differently on the basis of sex. 34 C.F.R. § 106.40(a).

34 C.F.R. § 106.40(b) specifically provides:

> (b) Pregnancy and related conditions. (1) A recipient shall not discriminate against any student, or exclude any student from its education program or activity, including any class or extracurricular activity, on the basis of such student's pregnancy, childbirth, false pregnancy, termination of pregnancy, or recovery therefrom, unless the student requests voluntarily to participate in a separate portion of the program or activity of the recipient.

The issue, then, is whether refusing to admit the plaintiffs to the GCNHS because they engaged in premarital sex and became pregnant constitutes exclusion "on the basis of pregnancy." Three prior cases have addressed the issue of exclusion from a NHS chapter due to pregnancy or premarital sexual activity.

Pregnancy Cannot Be the Criterion for Noninclusion

In the most recent of the three and the only circuit court decision on this issue, the court determined that the plaintiff was dismissed from the NHS not because she became pregnant but because she had engaged in premarital sex. *Pfeiffer v. Marion Ctr. Area Sch. Distr.*, (3rd Cir.1990). In *Pfeiffer* the court concluded that, as long as both genders were treated similarly with regard to premarital sex, the pregnant student could properly be dismissed from the NHS because "[r]egulation of conduct of unmarried high school student members is within the realm of authority of the National Honor Society given its emphasis on leadership and character." The court emphasized the requirement that the genders be treated similarly when it remanded the case to the trial court for consideration of testimony from a male student that he had fathered a child while a member of the NHS, yet had not been asked to resign from the chapter.

In an earlier case from the Central District of Illinois, the court reached a contrary conclusion. In *Wort v. Vierling*, (7th

Cir.1985), the court concluded that the plaintiff had been dismissed from the National Honor Society on the basis of her pregnancy rather than the premarital sex that resulted in the pregnancy. Therefore, because only women can become pregnant, the dismissal necessarily constituted unequal treatment based on gender and violated the Equal Protection Clause of the Fourteenth Amendment to the Constitution.

Finally, in *Cazares v. Barber,* (D.Ariz. May 31, 1990), the court encountered a relatively clear-cut case of gender discrimination. In that case, an otherwise eligible pregnant girl was denied entry into the NHS, but a male student who had fathered a child out of wedlock was accepted into the chapter. With little discussion, the court in that case determined that the plaintiff's denial of membership in the NHS violated both Title IX and the Fifth Amendment to the Constitution (the school in question was located on an Indian reservation and operated by the Bureau of Indian Affairs).

The court agrees with the two latter cases.

In the view of the court, based on the record now before it, plaintiffs' probability of successfully proving pregnancy discrimination is very high using either a disparate impact or disparate treatment method of proof.

Unintentional Discrimination Is Still Discrimination

The Title IX regulation quoted above unequivocally prohibits pregnancy discrimination by the defendants. Although its language is somewhat different, its purpose is generally the same as the Pregnancy Discrimination Act. Therefore, the court believes precedents under the Pregnancy Discrimination Act are applicable here.

Use of a disparate impact theory for proving discrimination is well recognized in pregnancy cases.

It has long been recognized that the anti-discrimination laws prohibit "both overt discrimination, as well as practices that are fair in form but discriminatory in operation." *U.S. v. City of Warren, Mich.*, (6th Cir.1998).

The plaintiff's burden in a disparate impact case "is to prove that a particular . . . practice has caused a significant adverse effect on a protected group. (Citations omitted) Once the plaintiff establishes the adverse effect, the burden shifts to the [defendant] to produce evidence that the challenged practice is a . . . necessity." *Id.*

It is not necessary to prove intentional discrimination when a disparate impact theory is used.

When a disparate impact analysis is applied to the evidence now of record in the instant case, the balance tips decidedly in favor of the plaintiffs.

The plaintiffs have met their burden of proving that the challenged practices of the defendants in screening students for admission to the NHS has caused a significant adverse effect on the protected group, i.e., young women who have become pregnant from premarital sex and have become visibly pregnant.

Statistically, 100% of such young women are not admitted to the GCNHS. Although the defendants argue that they are not basing their decision on pregnancy, but rather on non-marital sexual relations, the disparate impact on young women such as the plaintiffs is apparent.

Although 100% of young women who are visibly pregnant or who have had a child out of wedlock are denied membership, as far as the record reflects, defendants' policy excludes 0% of young men who have had premarital sexual relations and 0% of young women who have had such relations but have not become pregnant or have elected to have an early abortion.

The defendants claim that they would also exclude such students from the NHS membership but none have ever come to their attention. It may be that the discriminatory impact resulting from this policy is unintentional but, as stated above, proof of intentional discrimination is not required under a disparate impact theory.

In Chipman v. Grant County School District *(1998), a US district court in Kentucky ruled that high school students cannot be excluded from school activities such as the National Honor Society because they become pregnant.* © Lawrence Manning/Corbis.

The plaintiffs having met their initial burden of showing the significant adverse impact of defendants' policy, the burden now shifts to the defendants to show that the challenged practice is a reasonable necessity.

The defendants have not met such burden on the record now before the court. There are many alternate means to assess the character of candidates for membership in the NHS by non-discriminatory criteria.

Therefore the court holds that plaintiffs' probability of success herein is very high using a disparate impact theory.

Reasons for Exclusion Are Not Credible

The court also concludes that plaintiffs have a high probability of success on the more common disparate treatment theory.

Under this theory, a plaintiff seeking to prove discrimination must first prove that she is a member of a protected class who has been treated differently because of her sex or, in this case, because of pregnancy. Here, plaintiffs must prove they were treated differently than similarly situated non-pregnant students.

That these prerequisites have been met here is obvious.

The burden then shifts to the defendant to articulate legitimate, non-discriminatory reasons for its action. If the defendant is successful, the burden shifts back to the plaintiff to prove by a preponderance of the evidence that the non-discriminatory reason is a pretext for discrimination. The burden of persuasion, however, remains on the plaintiff throughout. If, however, the trier of the fact disbelieves the proffered non-discriminatory reason, it may draw an inference of discriminatory intent.

Considering solely the evidence in the present record, the court must find that the defendants here have failed to articulate a legitimate credible non-discriminatory reason for their NHS pregnancy policy. The reasons articulated for the exclusion of the plaintiffs are vague, conclusory and undocumented. In the face of the admitted fact that plaintiffs were the only students surpassing the grade cutoff who were excluded, the court on the present record finds these proffered non-discriminatory reasons insufficient and not credible. Therefore, an adverse inference of intentional discrimination arises.

Accordingly, the court finds that there is also a high likelihood of success on the merits by the plaintiffs under the disparate treatment theory.

In the light of the above analysis, the court finds it unnecessary to address the other issues raised by the parties.

NHS Membership Exclusion Will Cause Irreparable Injury

It is undisputed that this is the only time in these girls' lives that they will be seniors in high school with the opportunity to participate in NHS activities. Therefore, if an injunction does not issue, these girls will lose this opportunity forever. In addition, the plaintiffs will be unable to list NHS membership on their college admission applications and on financial aid applications. Accordingly, the plaintiffs will suffer some irreparable injury if the injunction does not issue. Also, the plaintiffs have undeniably suffered and are presently suffering emotional distress as a result of the defendants' policy.

The defendants contend that forcing them to admit plaintiffs to the GCNHS during the pendency of this action will deprive them of their right to enforce conduct in their schools that is consistent with the requirements of the various school activities. In addition, they contend, the public interest requires support of the public school's efforts to encourage high morals and strong character as part of the educational process. On the contrary, the plaintiffs note that the defendants are free to dismiss them from the NHS if this court ultimately determines that the defendants acted within their rights. Furthermore, the plaintiffs contend, it is always in the public interest to uphold the legal rights of others. The court holds the balance of equities favors the plaintiffs.

"The law requires schools to give all students who might be, are or have been pregnant . . . equal access to school programs and extracurricular activities."

Title IX Protects Pregnant and Parenting Students from Discrimination in School

National Women's Law Center

The National Women's Law Center is a Washington, DC–based nonprofit organization that conducts campaigns and spreads public awareness about the legal rights of women. In the following viewpoint, the Center describes how Title IX, an element of the 1972 Educational Amendments to the US Constitution, affords protection to female students who are pregnant or parenting. Title IX largely prohibits gender discrimination in public schools, and the National Women's Law Center contends that this policy preserves the rights of pregnant or parenting teens who seek to continue their education. The Law Center maintains that Title IX has been unfortunately overlooked or ignored by many school districts that routinely deny services to pregnant or parenting students. However, the organization insists that students can use the law to assist them in fighting discrimination and calls for school districts

National Women's Law Center, "A Pregnancy Test for Schools: The Impact of Education Laws on Pregnant and Parenting Students," 2012. Reproduced by permission.

to take note of the law and ensure that all students are given the chance to succeed.

The Equal Protection Clause of the Fourteenth Amendment to the U.S. Constitution prohibits sex discrimination, which includes discrimination based on sex-role stereotyping related to pregnancy or motherhood. In [*Nevada Department of Human Resources v. Hibbs* (2003)], the Supreme Court found that public employers violated the Constitution when they based employment policies on stereotypes about "mothers and mothers-to-be," including the notion that women should not work during certain stages of pregnancy. In some circumstances, pregnancy discrimination is also barred by the Constitution's Due Process Clause. The right to bear children is a fundamental one. In [*Cleveland Board of Education v. LaFleur* (1974)], the Supreme Court held that a blanket school board policy requiring all pregnant teachers to go on mandatory leave five months before their anticipated date of delivery violated the Due Process Clause because the "use of unwarranted conclusive presumptions . . . seriously burden[ed] the exercise of [a] protected constitutional liberty." The Court has also found that a blanket rule denying women unemployment benefits for twelve weeks before giving birth and six weeks afterwards violates the Due Process Clause because it "cannot be doubted that a substantial number of women are fully capable of working well into their last trimester of pregnancy and of resuming employment shortly after childbirth."

These same constitutional protections apply to pregnant and parenting students. Public schools are state actors bound by the Constitution's prohibition against sex discrimination. And discrimination based on overgeneralizations or stereotypes about pregnancy is sex discrimination, as are blanket presumptions that pregnant students are incapable of going to school, require remedial education, or that they should only attend separate programs. Sex-based discrimination in violation of the Constitution may be further demonstrated by the fact that such discrimination is typically targeted at pregnant and parenting female students, but not at similarly situated male students who father children.

The Protections Afforded Under Title IX

Title IX bans educational institutions that receive federal funds from discriminating against students based on their "actual or potential parental, family, or marital status" or a student's "pregnancy, childbirth, false pregnancy, termination of pregnancy or recovery therefrom." Generally speaking, this means that the law requires schools to give all students *who might be, are* or *have been* pregnant (whether currently parenting or not) equal access to school programs and extracurricular activities, and to treat pregnant and parenting students in the same way that they treat other students who are similarly able or unable to participate in school activities.

These protections mean that:

- Schools must provide equal access to school for pregnant and parenting students and treat pregnancy and all related conditions like any other temporary disability.

- Schools must provide equal access to extracurricular activities for pregnant and parenting students. For example, a school cannot require a doctor's note for pregnant students to participate in activities unless the school requires a doctor's note from all students who have conditions that require medical care.

- Absences due to pregnancy or childbirth must be excused for as long as deemed medically necessary by the student's doctor. The regulations require that at the conclusion of pregnancy-related leave, "a student must be reinstated to the status that she held when the leave began."

- If schools offer separate programs or schools for pregnant and parenting students, these programs must be voluntary and offer opportunities equal to those offered for non-pregnant students.

Title IX protects the rights of teen students who become pregnant. However, despite this protection, many schools ignore the statute and deny educational services to pregnant students. © Walter Lockwood/Corbis.

Examining Court Cases Related to Title IX

Although Title IX clearly protects the rights of pregnant and parenting students in high school, there have been very few court decisions related to the rights of pregnant and parenting secondary students. There are a number of reasons that these cases are so rare. First, many students and school officials are unaware that the law protects students from discrimination. Second, many young people may avoid lawsuits because of the financial and emotional costs, especially once they learn that a lawsuit may not offer the promise of immediate relief. Third, students who either reenroll in school or dropout may be unwilling to pursue claims. As such, the limited number of cases should not be interpreted to mean that schools are necessarily complying with Title IX.

The only published federal court cases regarding the application of Title IX to student pregnancy discrimination stem from high schools' denial of honor society membership to students who were or had been pregnant, either by refusing them admission in the first place, or by dismissing those who already were members. In the most recent example [as of 2012], *Chipman v. Grant County School District* [1998], two 17-year-old pregnant students with excellent grades—one with a GPA of 3.9 and one with a GPA of 3.7—were denied admission to the school's chapter of the National Honor Society [NHS], even though the other 31 students with GPAs of 3.5 or better were admitted. The girls and their families sued the school district under Title IX and the Equal Protection Clause. The school defended its action on the grounds that engaging in premarital sex and having a child out of wedlock made the girls ineligible due to the National Honor Society's "good character" requirement. The school argued that they based their decision on the fact that the girls had premarital sex, not on the fact that they were pregnant.

The district court forced the school to admit the girls to the honor society because the judge found no evidence that any male students had been excluded or dismissed for engaging in premarital sexual conduct. While the plaintiffs' pregnancies became obvious over time, the committee did not question any other applicants about their sexual histories. In another honor society case, there was evidence that male students who had fathered children out of wedlock were admitted to the NHS even though females were excluded. The plaintiffs in that case were able to show persuasively that defendants had violated Title IX and the Equal Protection Clause. And in another honor society case, the court of appeals instructed the trial court to consider evidence of whether the premarital sex policy was applied evenhandedly to male and female students.

Enforcing Title IX

The Department of Education's Office for Civil Rights (OCR) is tasked with enforcing Title IX, which includes reminding school districts of their civil rights obligations, assisting them with compliance, conducting investigations, and resolving complaints of discrimination. The role OCR plays in ensuring that school districts are attentive to and comply with Title IX's mandate against sex discrimination is key, but the most recent public education material issued by OCR on pregnant and parenting students is a pamphlet issued in July 1991.

OCR also has not used another important tool at its disposal; OCR's own records show that it has not undertaken proactive compliance reviews to determine to what extent schools are (or are not) in compliance with the law as it applies to pregnant and parenting students. OCR could, for example, compare the course offerings available to students in alternative programs with those in mainstream schools or it could review local homebound and absence policies to assess their impact on pregnant students. In addition to compliance reviews, OCR also maintains an administrative complaint procedure. But only a handful of students actually file complaints because few people know the option exists and the time it takes for OCR to fully investigate and resolve complaints can extend beyond the point the students at issue have given birth, graduated, or dropped out.

Federal Assistance Services Are Limited

Although the definition of "at-risk students" in state and federal law is sometimes broad enough to include pregnant and parenting students, funding designated broadly for at-risk youth often does not make its way to pregnant and parenting students. For example, Title I Part D of the Elementary and Secondary Education Act is a grant program for "neglected, delinquent, and at-risk youth." Pregnant and parenting students are identified in the definition of youth who are at-risk, but given the discretion to spend funds on any at-risk population, many school districts will choose not to invest in their pregnant and parenting students. And the federal government does not track how these funds are spent, so it is impossible to determine just how much of each local educational agency's expenditure is spent on

Complying with Title IX Requires a Change in Attitude

While schools without adequate funding for all students will have a difficult time accommodating students with special needs, it is important to stress that some of the mandates of Title IX do not require more funding, but simply—or perhaps not so simply—a change of attitude toward pregnant and mothering students to provide equitable school experiences for women. . . . Why is it considered "indecent" to show a pregnant extended belly at school? What attitudes underscore the desire to conceal the pregnant students in alternative programs? Why do pregnant bodies not belong in student bodies? It does not cost money to provide keys to elevators, to allow students with swollen ankles to arrive a few minutes late to class, or even to allow students with morning sickness the option of being able to eat during class. The raised eyebrows, tsk-tsk dismissals, and insensitive commands to "just hold it" send these young women the message that they do not belong in the classroom, at the prom, or in the Honor Society. Schools are required, by law, to create a culture that does not stigmatize pregnant and mothering students, and without discounting the larger structural realities, the narratives of too many of the young mothers in this study suggest that they still experience hostile school environments.

Mary Patrice Erdmans, "Title IX and the School Experiences of Pregnant and Mothering Students," Humanity and Society, *2012.*

students who are pregnant or parenting versus students who are at risk for other reasons.

There are a number of other federal programs that are specifically aimed at implementing Title IX or improving outcomes for pregnant and parenting students. These programs include the Women's Educational Equity Act, Adolescent Family Life Demonstration Project, and the Pregnancy Assistance Fund.

Funding for these programs, however, is extremely limited relative to the need and drastically narrows what they can accomplish. For example, the Department of Health and Human Services administers the Pregnancy Assistance Fund (PAF), which provides $25 million in competitive grants to 17 states. PAF grantees are charged with providing pregnant and parenting women with a network of supportive services to help them complete high school or postsecondary degrees and gain access to health care, child care, family housing, and other critical supports. While many of the PAF grantees have developed promising programs, the grants go to a limited number of states and most of those states can offer services to a limited number of students.

Title IX Is Often Overlooked

While federal law clearly prohibits discrimination against pregnant and parenting students, this aspect of Title IX has not received enough attention and discrimination persists around the country. In 1981, a national study of alternative programs for pregnant students found that "Title IX had little effect on the school site policies" and that "many regular school staff were not aware of [Title IX's] implications for student pregnancy and parenthood." The same could be said today. Unfortunately, many schools and districts do not inform parents and students about Title IX and fail to meet even the most basic requirement of appointing a Title IX coordinator. On top of a lack of awareness, enforcement of Title IX has not focused on this area. A serious public education and enforcement effort is required to root out discrimination against pregnant and parenting students.

Finally, even though Title IX sets the floor—barring discrimination against pregnant and parenting students—schools and districts are uniquely positioned to go beyond the federal law by providing additional support and encouragement that can improve pregnant and parenting students' chances for success.

| *"Teen parents in schools are discriminated against not only by their peers, but primarily by school staff."*

A Woman Who Became a Teen Mother Describes the Bullying She Endured from High School Teachers and Staff

Natasha Vianna

Natasha Vianna was a young mother when she attended high school. In the following viewpoint, Vianna describes how difficult it was for her to get the support she needed from educators in order to balance her schoolwork with parenting. Vianna claims she was a good student, but her teachers had unreasonably low expectations for her success simply because she chose to have a child at a young age. She relates several instances in which school staff demeaned her for her pregnancy or showed little tolerance for her needs as a young mother. She advises all young mothers to know their rights and protections in the face of educational discrimination. Vianna is now the Teen Parent Ambassador Coordinator for Brigham Women's Hospital in Boston and a freelance writer.

The teen pregnancy prevention ads making headlines in New York City are offensive and are a part of a system that consistently degrades teen moms. What these public service announcements promote is a continuation of the unfair treatment of the young women who need support. It enables those who have personal agenda against teen moms to effectively use their disapproval to make their lives MUCH harder than it needs to be.

Stereotyping Young Mothers

When teens become parents, they instantly become victims of discrimination, judgment, and stereotyping. They are expected to drop out of high school, apply for welfare, neglect their children, and accomplish nothing to be proud of. For most teen parents, expecting a child comes with stares, negative comments, mistreatment, and bullying. Without a doubt, teen parents in schools are discriminated against not only by their peers, but primarily by school staff.

What happens when the very people who are supposed to ensure you are in a safe and stable learning environment are the ones making your education a depressing experience? I can tell you what that's like because it happened to me.

Driven Out of School

At 17, I discovered I was pregnant. Nervous, anxious, upset, and scared were the beginning of how I felt during the first few weeks of secrecy. After missing many days of school from morning sickness and prenatal appointments, I decided it was time to tell my school nurse about my pregnancy. Her disappointed tone and bitter lips asked me if I considered an abortion, and when I said yes but decided not to get one, she looked away in disbelief. By the end of the week, all of my teachers knew I was pregnant. Some gave me puppy dog eyes but said nothing, some avoided eye contact when I asked to use the bathroom, and one pulled me aside to tell me that I made a huge mistake. The students gossiped, but they did it behind my back and without me knowing. The teachers, oh the teachers, they showed their disapproval to my face.

I couldn't handle it. I was the only girl in my school who was having a baby, but not the only girl who got pregnant because some chose to leave secretly and others aborted. I finished the school year and transferred to a different school. My new school was much larger and had a much higher number of pregnant and parenting students. While I was nervous to be the new girl (who was already 6 months pregnant by the beginning of the school year), I was happy to know there would be a better support system during my senior year of school. My new high school had a health clinic and a designated liaison who worked with teen moms in the school. I never realized how much of a pivotal role in my life this woman would make.

Schools Have Low Expectations for Teen Mothers

The teachers knew nothing about me prior to my first day. All they knew was that I was new at the school and pregnant. Their expectations were extremely low. After my first day of school, I went to my guidance counselor's office to ask why I was no longer in honors classes. The classes were boring and slow-paced and covered materials I already knew. Her response was that she questioned whether I would even graduate high school so it would be safer to put me in easy classes that I could easily pass versus putting me in challenging classes. In shock, I walked away from her office. I came back two months later to ask her if she would help me apply for college, she told me that it would be best to focus on graduating school—then if I did, maybe I could enroll into a community college. Again, I walked away with my head hung low.

The subtle events were a little bit easier to tolerate and move on from but there were some blatant moments of discrimination that made me want to burst into tears. When I returned back to school from maternity leave in February of 2006, I made the decision to exclusively breastfeed my child. I would carve out two 20 minute sessions of my day to pump milk in the nurse's office while my classmates enjoyed their homeroom and lunch periods. Apparently, one of my teachers thought this was a way for me to escape student life and avoid the work that all other classmates were doing. She would refuse to let me leave her class if my breasts were engorged. Intimidated, I didn't argue. One day, as I sat in her class with swollen breasts and extreme discomfort, I raised my hand and asked her if I could leave. She said no, I begged, she said no. A few moments later, my breasts began to leak. I was wearing breast pads but I was so full that they began to leak through the pads. The teacher looked over at me, pointed in front of a class of 18 year olds, and said "You're leaking breast-milk." My face turning beet red, I ran out of the room and cried in the nurse's office.

Teachers Ignore the Needs of Young Mothers

This wasn't the only incident. I missed a lot of school and it infuriated my teachers. What annoyed them the most was that my absences were legitimately excused. After returning to school one day after an absence, I handed my teacher my doctor's note. She looked at it, looked at me, and asked why I had to miss an entire day of school because of one appointment. I told her my daughter had an appointment. She almost laughed and told me that appointments don't take 8 hours. Furiously, she told me that I would HAVE to come after school to take the quiz I missed. I agreed. She reminded me, in front of my entire class, that I CHOSE to become a teen mom in high school and that I would not get special treatment. As I sat in my chair, I thought about all the things I wanted to say to her. See, she didn't know my daughter was also born with congenital hypothyroidism. We spent days in the hospital before she was even a week old. During infancy, we were in the hospital on a weekly basis for the first few months and with blood tests, labs, and several visits to different specialists, appointments DID take 8 hours. And as an 18-year-old balancing school and parenthood, this was in no way easier than taking a math quiz. School was much easier than my home life. But I didn't say anything. I came after school and aced my quiz. It was the only way I knew how to piss her off.

School was hell for me. When the teachers don't want to see you succeed, you feel as if your mere presence in the school is unwanted. I genuinely felt as though my success and my good grades angered the people who wanted to prove that teen parenthood put young people on a path to failure or that their scare tactic would become null and void if I became the teen mom who graduated and went to college. It was the only explanation.

The Law Protects Against Discrimination

We know that bullying has become an issue for students. There isn't one person who is more likely to be bullied than another and as a whole society, we agree that students should have access to education without the worry that they will be discriminated against or bullied. Yet, it happens every single day. Teen parents are no exception to this rule. If school staff and "support" people are purposely making a teen parent's life harder and making it more difficult for young parents to acquire an education, they are violating Title IX rights and are BULLIES.

Title IX protects all students attending schools that receive any federal funding (all public schools receive some federal funding) from discrimination on the basis of your sex or on the basis of pregnancy, childbirth, false pregnancy, termination of pregnancy or recovery therefrom

> *"I believe the girls who find themselves in these circumstances can fulfill their dreams and aspirations with the right amount of determination and guidance."*

Teen Mothers Should Not Drop Out of School

Philoron Wright

Philoron Wright asserts in the following viewpoint that teen motherhood is a challenge to academic growth. She argues that she sees too many girls forsaking their educations to meet the trials of parenting. However, Wright claims that school programs exist to help young mothers continue their studies while pregnant or raising a child. Wright believes education is the key to a better life, and she encourages teen mothers to stay in school and seek the assistance they need to succeed. Wright is an assistant to the superintendent of community and schools in Alachua, Florida.

In recent weeks [December 2012] I have had the opportunity to meet five pregnant teenage girls and mothers. I was struck by the different paths they chose for their futures. Two of the girls I met have decided to stay in school along with a young teenage mother who is also in school. These three girls seem to share the same goal, and that is to earn a high school diploma.

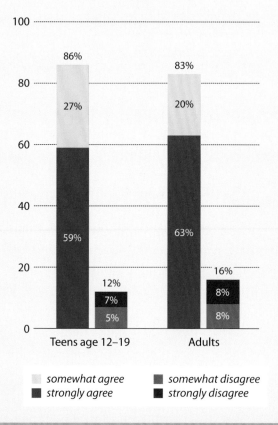

Teen Pregnancy and Education

How much do you agree or disagree with the following statement: "Reducing teen pregnancy is a very effective way to reduce the high school dropout rate and improve academic achievement."

Taken from: Bill Albert, *With One Voice 2012: America's Adults and Teens Sound Off About Teen Pregnancy*. Washington, DC: National Campaign to Prevent Teen and Unplanned Pregnancy, August 2012.

On the other hand, two other pregnant girls I met a couple of days ago decided that dropping out of school was best for them, and they have no desire to return to school. In the short time I spent with them trying to convince them to return to school, I saw little interest.

They were accepting of their situation and expressed shallow reasons for not returning. Several thoughts went through my head as I spoke to these girls. Will she get the support she needs from the father of the child? What kind of life will the child have? And why is education not a priority? There were so many unanswered questions for me.

Developing an Education Plan

I wish to acknowledge that in no way am I passing judgment on these girls and their circumstances. Many of us have faced situations that altered our paths and which may have resulted in putting our education on hold.

All five of these young girls seem to be bright, beautiful, healthy and caring individuals. Nothing about them would suggest that they could not have a successful, productive life. However, the two girls who were not in school do not seem to have a plan, other than depending on the support of their moms and grandmothers.

In this [viewpoint] I clearly want to emphasize that opportunities for furthering one's education are available for young mothers and pregnant teenage girls. These girls must understand that there is life beyond their circumstances of motherhood.

Education can continue even while they are raising a child. The path to a better life is through education, and there are so many ways they can achieve their goals. The key is not to give up.

Programs to Help Young Mothers

In Alachua County [in Gainesville, Florida] we have the Accept Program, which allows young pregnant girls to continue their education. This program is part of the Loften Center High School. Their emphasis is geared toward a strong academic curriculum and preparing young girls for their new roles as mothers.

The school's program helps young girls focus on getting a diploma and prepares them for college eligibility and career tech programs. These programs will provide opportunities for

Although attending school as a teen parent can be difficult, opportunities are available for young mothers to continue their education. Some high schools provide childcare to help parenting teens. © Mika/Corbis.

employment. So there are career path classes that will meet the needs of these students. Again, the key is to stay in school and not give up.

In this [viewpoint] I dare not speak on the morality of a girl's decision to get pregnant, but I will address the matter that there are consequences. I'm sure by now these young mothers-to-be and teenage mothers know that having a child is a full-time responsibility that requires constant care. With this in mind it is very hard to juggle school and provide care for their young child at the same time.

At the Loften Center there is a child care center for students attending Loften so they can continue their education. Every person should know by now that knowledge is power, and it is greatly needed by young pregnant teenage girls and mothers more so than their counterparts

It is imperative in this day and age that our young teenage mothers be able to find the resources they need to care for their young children. This is where education is vital.

Teen Mothers Need Determination to Continue Their Education

I have known so many young girls who found themselves in a parental role at an early age who completed the Loften Program and are doing well. It takes discipline, courage and motivation to see a dream come true. I believe the girls who find themselves in these circumstances can fulfill their dreams and aspirations with the right amount of determination and guidance.

If you are one of these girls who have dropped out of school and are facing motherhood, allow me to encourage you to go back to school. It may be a challenge for you, but it is worth the effort.

In addition, it would be wise and prudent for teenage girls to practice birth control or abstinence to avoid compromising their dreams and goals. The responsibility of raising children can be an obstacle for teenage mothers to achieve success.

For the upcoming semester and school year, I would ask these young teenagers to find a way back to enter the doors of a school.

Enjoy the holidays and always love your children.

| "A few states have developed programs to help improve graduate rates among pregnant girls and young mothers."

Schools Can Help Teen Mothers Achieve a Better Education

Kelli Kennedy

In the following viewpoint, Kelli Kennedy reports on school-based educational assistance to pregnant girls and young parents. Kennedy contends that while some schools expect teen parents to be low-achievers and do little to aid them in graduating, others are implementing programs to improve attendance, provide busing and child care, and send home assignments to homebound students. According to Kennedy, such programs are helping many teens graduate while also allowing them to care for their children. She warns, however, that budget cuts threaten the continuance of assistance efforts, jeopardizing the futures of these young parents. Kennedy is an Associated Press writer who covers social services news in Miami.

When 15-year-old Kali Gonzalez became pregnant, the honors student considered transferring to an alternative

Kelli Kennedy, "Teen Pregnancy Study: Students Need Better School Support," Associated Press, November 22, 2012. Reprinted with permission of the Associated Press.

school. She worried teachers would harass her for missing class because of doctor's appointments and morning sickness.

A guidance counselor urged Gonzalez not to, saying that could lower her standards.

Instead, her counselor set up a meeting with teachers at her St. Augustine high school to confirm she could make up missed assignments, eat in class and use the restroom whenever she needed. Gonzalez, who is now 18, kept an A-average while pregnant. She capitalized on an online school program for parenting students so she could stay home and take care of her baby during her junior year. She returned to school her senior year and graduated with honors in May.

But Gonzalez is a rare example of success among pregnant students. Schools across the country are divided over how to handle them, with some schools kicking them out or penalizing students for pregnancy-related absences. And many schools say they can't afford costly support programs, including tutoring, child care and

Online programs for parenting students help them keep up with their studies while taking care of their child. Many support programs for teenage parents are in jeopardy, as school districts across the country face budgetary challenges. © Ingo Bartussek/Fotolia.com.

transportation for teens who may live just a few miles from school but still too far to walk while pregnant or with a small child.

Nearly 400,000 girls and young women between 15 and 19 years old gave birth in 2010, a rate of 34 per 1,000, according to the Centers for Disease Control and Prevention.

Budget Cuts Impact Programs for Pregnant and Parenting Teens

Those statistics have led child advocates to push for greater adherence to a 1972 law that bans sex discrimination in federally funded education programs and activities, according to a new report by the National Women's Law Center.

Fatima Goss Graves, the center's vice president of education and employment, says offering pregnant teens extra support would ultimately save taxpayers money by helping them become financially independent and not dependent on welfare.

But budget cuts have eaten into such efforts.

California lawmakers slashed a successful program for such students in 2008, ruling it was no longer mandatory, and allowed school districts to use the money for other programs.

More than 100,000 pregnant and parenting students have participated in the program that helps them with classwork and connects them with social services. It boasted a 73 percent graduation rate in 2010—close to the state's normal rate—and advocates said participants were less reliant on welfare and less likely to become pregnant again. That compares to several counties where only 30 percent of pregnant and parenting teens graduated. "It's unfortunate that this effective program fell prey to the enormous budget challenges we are facing as a state," said State Superintendent of Public Instruction Tom Torlakson.

State Policies Vary

Three years ago in Wisconsin, cost-cutting lawmakers dropped a requirement for school districts to give pregnant students who live within two miles of a school building free rides to school.

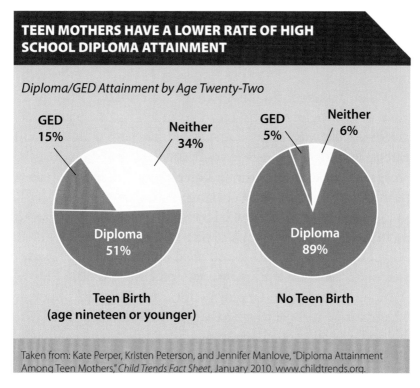

TEEN MOTHERS HAVE A LOWER RATE OF HIGH SCHOOL DIPLOMA ATTAINMENT

Diploma/GED Attainment by Age Twenty-Two

GED 15% Neither 34% Diploma 51%

Teen Birth (age nineteen or younger)

GED 5% Neither 6% Diploma 89%

No Teen Birth

Taken from: Kate Perper, Kristen Peterson, and Jennifer Manlove, "Diploma Attainment Among Teen Mothers," *Child Trends Fact Sheet*, January 2010. www.childtrends.org.

The requirement had been part of an effort to improve access to education and reduce infant mortality rates.

Less than half of the states have programs that send home assignments to homebound or hospitalized student parents, according to the study.

In almost half of the states, including Idaho, Nevada, Nebraska, South Dakota and Utah, the definition of excused absences is not broad enough to include pregnant and parenting students. That typically results in a patchwork of policies where some school districts don't excuse absences even if the student is in the hospital giving birth, according to the study.

Improving Graduation Rates for Pregnant Teens and Young Parents

But a few states have developed programs to help improve graduate rates among pregnant girls and young mothers.

In Washington, D.C., caseworkers in the New Heights Teen Parent Program often stand by the school entrance or text pregnant students and young moms to make sure they are attending classes.

When students do miss school, caseworkers take them homework assignments. About 600 students participate in the program which also helps students with housing, child care and parenting skills. But the $1.6 million federal grant funding the program runs out next year and officials said they don't have a clear future funding source.

Roughly 4,500 male and female student parents participated in a Pennsylvania program last year [2011] where case workers helped them balance school and child care. Nearly 1,300 graduated or received an equivalent, state officials said. The ELECT [Education Leading to Employment Career Training] program, which started in 1990 as a partnership between state child welfare and education officials, monitors students' attendance, coordinates summer programs and links them with support systems in the community.

Florida allows pregnant and parenting students to receive homebound instruction and lays out a clear process to make up missed work. The state also gives those students the option of taking online classes.

In St. Johns County, where Gonzalez lives, the school district provides free day care for teen moms and bus transportation for students and their children.

Pregnant students are often stereotyped as low-achievers, but advocates say pregnancy actually motivates some to do better in school.

Gonzalez, whose daughter is now 2, said her grades improved after she became pregnant.

"I did push myself a lot harder and I made sure that I wasn't going to be that statistic," said Gonzalez, who is now married and pursuing a nursing degree.

10

> "Education seemed to be the key—the missing piece of an old and complicated puzzle I had been trying to solve throughout my life."

A Woman Who Became a Mother at Thirteen Reflects on the Importance of Education

Sherita Rooney

Sherita Rooney is an African American mother who persisted in her academic studies while raising two young children. Giving birth to her first child at age thirteen, Rooney eventually attended college and utilized the support system the school offered to keep up her grades and acquire the financial aid necessary to continue her education. Focusing on bettering herself for the sake of her children, Rooney is now working slowly toward a degree in mathematics, preparing to become a teacher to serve high school students from underprivileged backgrounds. Rooney is currently a student at West Chester University in Pennsylvania.

From where I sit mine isn't a sad story, nor is it unique. A picture of my life would resemble that of many American girls, painted with slightly different strokes and a few highlighted

Sherita Rooney, "Unlocking the Door to Life's Possibilities," *On Campus with Women*, Winter 2012. Reproduced by permission.

blessings. Although I have experienced many things during my twenty-nine years, in a sense the life I lead today began at one distinctive moment: when I learned that I was pregnant.

I was thirteen years old and in the eighth grade when I discovered that I, although still a child myself, would soon be raising a child of my own. At that point in my life, I lacked a clear vision for my future. Having recently received the devastating news that I had not been accepted into the prestigious all-girls school I had dreamed of attending, I was now confronted with the challenge of creating not only an alternative plan for my education, but also one for my life as a teenage mother.

Choosing to Pursue an Education

When I discovered that I was pregnant, I evaluated the world around me for the first time. I had never thought much about where I was headed in the long term, but now I dreamed of a bright future for my unborn child. In the past, skipping school, getting drunk, and doing drugs seemed not only normal, but like legitimate ways to deal with the challenges of growing up in a poor neighborhood without many opportunities. But as I began to think outside of my immediate circumstances, I saw that would have to change. I wondered how I could help my child escape the seemingly inevitable patterns around me. If I could complete my education, I decided, I would be able to provide for my child and perhaps show him or her how much there is to life.

Education seemed to be the key—the missing piece of an old and complicated puzzle I had been trying to solve throughout my life. Most of my immediate family had been unable to continue their education past grade school, and they worked in low-paying service-oriented jobs as a result. My mother had enrolled in college, but dropped out when she became pregnant with her first child. Growing up, I watched her struggle to raise seven children alone and on welfare, working three jobs to take care of us. Despite her hard work, we often had to go without heat or electricity. At a young age, I began to abhor being poor and saw

A Renewed Interest in Education

Teenage parents have described how having a child reinforced their interest in education and was instrumental in helping them to see how education would help them provide a better future for their children, increase their employment possibilities, and help them avoid depending on public assistance. The decision to accept available support is characterized as the personal transformation stage of teenage parenting. The personal transformation stage begins when a teenage mother realizes that success and freedom for her and her child do not come without personal drive, unselfish dedication, and a commitment to succeed.

Ann Neeley et al., "Teenage Parents and Their Educational Attainment," Texas Comprehensive Center at SEDL, 2011. http://txcc.sedl.org.

a lack of proper education as the common denominator among people of low socioeconomic class status.

What if I could break the pattern and graduate from college? With this question in mind, education became my stabilizer, my pathway to life's possibilities. I enrolled in courses at Pennsylvania's Montgomery County Community College when my daughter had reached the tender age of four. I knew she was silently learning from my choices. This time I would try my best to make the right ones.

Getting Help from College Services

Fortunately, I have been able to stay the course, thanks to assistance I received as a student. When my grades began to decline in my very first semester, I was contacted by representatives from the college's Act 101 Program (named for the Pennsylvania law passed in 1971). This was exactly what I needed at the time. I had no idea how to navigate the college process: how to study, how to write a paper, or even how to schedule my classes. Act 101 counselors helped with these aspects and even stayed in contact with my professors to monitor my attendance. They helped keep track of my grades and offered me tutoring in my most challenging classes. Before each semester, I made an appointment with a counselor who would help me schedule my classes. Counselors also held meetings in a relaxed setting where Act 101 students could discuss our struggles, life experiences, and goals for the future. The women who led the program became my mentors and confidants. Their assistance was invaluable to my progress as a student.

Approximately five years later, after having my second child, I joined the college's Keys Program. At this point I had been in school for almost ten years, having taken only one or two classes each semester while working more than thirty hours a week to make ends meet. The Keys Program provided critical financial aid that helped offset my expenses for daycare, books, and transportation. As a single parent with a ten-year-old daughter and a one-year-old son, I was in dire need of this assistance. Along with the housing voucher program, it allowed me to quit my job and focus on finally finishing my associate's degree.

The Act 101 program and the Keys Program gave me the practical assistance I needed to succeed as a student. Just as important, being involved in them helped me feel connected to the school community. I became more engaged in other organizations on campus, including the African American Student League, the African Student Association, and the Meridian Club (an organization for nontraditional students, which I had the privilege of leading as president in its fortieth year). I thus became a leader on campus as I proceeded toward graduation.

I graduated from Montgomery County Community College after making the dean's list for several consecutive semesters. Following graduation, I transferred to West Chester University to continue my education. I hope to obtain my bachelor's degree in math education in May 2013 and to teach mathematics to underserved high school students whose stories resemble to my own.

Using Education to Serve Others

As I prepare to become a teacher, I hope to build confidence and gain knowledge that I can use to support excellence in education for minorities and the underprivileged. My journey has shown me that education is the pathway to so many wonderful things. By obtaining my degree, I hope to not only enrich my own life and the lives of my fifteen-year-old daughter and six-year-old son, but also those of many voiceless children whom I believe deserve a chance.

In pursuing this goal, I am inspired by the many accomplished African American thinkers whom I have had the privilege of meeting over the course of my education. Learning about their struggles and successes has shown me not only the sheer tenacity that they possess, but also the endurance I have within myself. I have a fire in me now that will never be extinguished.

> "These schools appear to work, in large
> part, because the staff maintains an
> intense sense of purpose and because
> students with similar life circumstances
> band together."

The Miracle of Polly McCabe

Jake Halpern

In the following viewpoint, Jake Halpern relates the success of alternative schools for pregnant teens by focusing on a young girl who attended the Polly T. McCabe Center in New Haven, Connecticut. According to Halpern, the McCabe Center caters exclusively to pregnant girls, providing both educational instruction and prenatal care. The young girl Halpern interviews describes the center as a welcoming place in which counselors are focused on helping their students get degrees and succeed in life. Halpern explains that such facilities offer a safe haven for pregnant teens who are often made to feel like outsiders at public schools. Halpern's works include a pair of nonfiction titles and the Dormia *trilogy of fantasy novels. His articles have appeared in publications such as the* New York Times, *the* Wall Street Journal, *and* GQ.

Nancy is a quiet Mexican-American girl who lives in New Haven. She has shoulder-length black hair, sleepy brown eyes, and, for a time, wore a silver stud pierced just beneath her

Jake Halpern, "The Miracle of Polly McCabe," first appeared in the *Boston Globe*, February 27, 2011. Copyright © 2011 by Jake Halpern.

bottom lip. In late 2009, when Nancy was 14 years old, she discovered she was pregnant.

Shortly before, Nancy and her 16-year-old sister, Diana, had
gone to stay with their aunt in New York City. Nancy's mother,
Sandra, was an illegal immigrant who had recently returned to
Mexico to visit an ailing family member. It was unclear when or
how she would get back to the United States.

The arrangement at the aunt's house worked out fine for a
while, up until Nancy got pregnant. "My aunt didn't want me
having the baby—she said, 'If you want the baby, you can't live
here,'" Nancy recalled. (This story uses just the first or middle
names to protect minors' identities.) Her aunt thought having a
baby would ruin Nancy's life, that she couldn't possibly be pregnant and stay in school. So she told Nancy she needed to pick a
date to get an abortion.

"I didn't know what to do," Nancy told me. "I didn't have any
money, I didn't know anybody, and my mom wasn't there." In a
panic, she stuffed her things into a backpack, borrowed money
from an uncle, and took a bus back to New Haven.

Nancy hid out at a friend's house and stopped attending
school. A few weeks later, she heard from her estranged father.
He invited Nancy and Diana to move into his New Haven apartment. Nancy hadn't spoken to her father in three years, but she
needed a place to stay. Plus, he lived just a few blocks away from
John, the 15-year-old father of her baby.

For a time, Nancy's life felt relatively stable. She was living with
her father, and her sister had joined them from New York. But she
still had no idea when she would be able to return to school.

One evening still early in her pregnancy, she was shopping
for maternity clothing at Walmart when she began to have heavy
vaginal bleeding. She remembers thinking she was about to lose
the baby. She rushed to Yale-New Haven Hospital, where the
doctors assured her that both she and the baby were OK.

Afterward, a nurse asked Nancy about her plans for the
future—would she return to school? Nancy wasn't sure how she

could. The nurse handed her a piece of paper with a phone number for a nearby alternative school named Polly McCabe. Nancy called, and a week later she was a student again.

A School for Pregnant Girls

The Polly T. McCabe Center is a public school that enrolls only one type of student: pregnant girls like Nancy. Some of the teens appear old beyond their years, with faded flowery tattoos winding up their arms; others are self-conscious, fretting over stretch marks more than pimples. The staff at McCabe, led by principal Bernadette Strode, strives to keep students in school and simultaneously teach them to be good mothers. The girls get door-to-door bus service, on-site child care, classes on child rearing, in-school visits from prenatal experts, intensive support from case workers, and even home visits from teachers if they go on bed rest.

The idea behind McCabe is not just to help teen mothers, but also to fight poverty. According to the latest national figures from Child Trends, a nonpartisan research center, 43 percent of girls who have babies before age 18 don't earn high school diplomas or GEDs by the time they're 22. This, of course, severely limits their prospects for economic advancement.

Nationally, pregnancy is the leading cause of teen girls dropping out of high school. According to the Massachusetts Alliance on Teen Pregnancy, more than 2,000 new mothers and fathers in this state leave school each year. Local officials say they want to cut that dropout rate in half by 2014, but Boston has only one school devoted entirely to pregnant teens—St. Mary's Alternative School in Dorchester—and it has the capacity for only 20 students (less than half as many as the McCabe Center). That's not many spots, given the fact that Boston has more than 500 new teen mothers each year.

A Push to Mainstream All Students

A few decades ago, there were almost 300 "pregnancy schools" like St. Mary's and McCabe across the country. But starting in the late 1970s, the federal government began to slash funding for them, and many have closed. New York City, for instance, shut down its four schools in 2007. To some, the idea of separate schools for distinct groups—especially disadvantaged ones— seemed a little too much like segregation. "The students who got shipped off to these schools were poor students of color who already had gaps in their education," says Benita Miller, executive director of the nonprofit Brooklyn Young Mothers' Collective. When Miller visited one now-shuttered school in Brooklyn, she was surprised to see students not studying, but taking naps and knitting baby blankets.

Many educators instead embraced the virtues of "mainstreaming," where all students, no matter their circumstances, shared one experience.

But Lisa Miller, a professor at Columbia University's Teachers College, thinks the mainstreaming movement has gone too far. She says she studied students at New York's onetime pregnancy schools and witnessed a kind of education that defies normal academic benchmarks. During one group therapy session Miller attended, a student confessed that she couldn't afford diapers— much less anything else her baby would need. The baby's father was in a gang, though, and other gang members' girlfriends had offered to throw her a lavish baby shower, but only if she swore her newborn into the gang. "The girls in the therapy session confronted her and got through to her in a way that couldn't be matched by any therapist," Miller says. The girl ended up forging a relationship with her boyfriend's mother, who bought her what she needed. In the mainstream model, Miller says, "I can't envision a space where pregnant girls could redirect their lives like this."

Some educators have recently begun re-entertaining the notion that there may be distinct benefits to niche schools. Several states, for instance, educate former drug and alcohol abusers at so-called "sober schools." In Illinois, there are three Urban Prep Academies—all-male, mostly African-American charter high

Alternative schools can offer a safe environment and special services for pregnant teens that may not exist in regular schools. © Yellow Dog Productions/The Image Bank/Getty Images.

schools. Last spring, the Urban Prep program graduated its first class—all 107 students were headed to college.

These schools appear to work, in large part, because the staff maintains an intense sense of purpose and because students with similar life circumstances band together. "A school is only 50 percent a curricular space—it is every bit as much a psychological space," Miller concludes. "Some students have very specific needs that can only be met through the psychological space of the school, and, for these students, mainstreaming can work against them."

Combining Child Care and Coursework

Nancy arrived at McCabe on a bleak December morning in 2009, when she was nearly five months pregnant. Initially, she came across as polite but guarded. "I have seen people beaten down mentally—without hope—but I didn't see that with her," says Strode, the school's principal. "I remember saying to Nancy's case manager, 'There is something here that is hidden.'"

One member of the McCabe staff told me that the key to motivating students is "gentle nagging"—asking them every day whether they've done their homework or perhaps obtained a car seat for their baby. Yet, according to Strode, the key is for students themselves to believe both that they belong there and that the school can really help them.

McCabe devotes much of its resources to two areas: providing in-school child care for the new mothers and keeping class sizes very small. A student named Bernice told me that she could never make sense of the periodic table in chemistry class at her previous school: "When I came here, the periodic table just seemed to make sense and fly by with no problem at all. The teacher could stop and break it down. I am now in a class of six or four, as opposed to being in a class of 27. I can say, 'Excuse me, I need help understanding this,' and they can stop and explain, which they couldn't do at my old school."

Nancy also seemed to benefit from the personal attention at McCabe. Her homeroom teacher, Elizabeth Bradshaw, told me that one day Nancy confided that she had never learned how to read a newspaper. Bradshaw showed her how the stories from the front page were continued in other sections. "After that, every day she read the whole paper, cover to cover, everything from the cartoons to the Op-Eds," Bradshaw said. Nancy's art teacher, Brigitte London, praised her artwork and encouraged her to submit it to several shows and competitions.

An Impressive Educational Track Record

There is, however, more than just anecdotal evidence to suggest that McCabe is effective. Two researchers at Yale University, Victoria Seitz and Nancy Apfel, studied a group of students who attended McCabe in the early 1980s and tracked their progress for 18 years. They found that the longer nearly failing students

stayed at McCabe, the more academically successfully they became. For the students who spent one academic quarter there,
17 percent had either graduated or were on track to do so two
years later. For those who stayed four quarters, that number
jumped to 80 percent.

The school's track record remains impressive today [2011].
At the national level, only 38 percent of young mothers graduate
from high school by age 22, and even fewer go to college. But last
year, 80 percent of McCabe students graduated, and 50 percent
were looking forward to filling out their college applications.

What makes McCabe work? What's at the core of its success?
It could be the small class sizes or the staff's "gentle nagging," but
it could also be the school's esprit de corps—the sense of common purpose and belonging that its students feel. Donna Ford of
Vanderbilt University, who studies student underachievement,
describes this phenomenon as a "cohort effect." She explains:
"When you take a cohort of kids with similar needs and issues
and put them in a safe haven—without any distractions—it
makes all the difference in the world."

Nancy made this same point to me on several occasions.
"The best thing about being [at McCabe] is that nobody judges
you—nobody puts you down for being pregnant," she said. "We
all understand each other; we are all going through similar
situations."

What Nancy said really resonated for me during a class field
trip. Last May [2010], high school students from around New
Haven had been invited to see a matinee of *A Doll's House*, by
Henrik Ibsen. Nancy and some of her classmates were bused to
the theater, and as we pulled into the parking lot, we saw several
hundred students milling around. Almost all of them were white,
and none appeared pregnant. A few McCabe students stood up
as if to leave the bus, then sat back down. Outside, many of the
other kids just kept staring.

"Don't look at our bus!" one of the McCabe students yelled
out the window.

Another McCabe student chimed in, "I used to be that skinny!"

"They look at you like, 'Why'd you do this?'" one girl told me. "Like they would never have done it."

Eventually, the McCabe girls exited the bus, entered the theater, and headed en masse to the bathroom, where they stayed for a long time before finally taking their seats.

The play was a success. When the McCabe students were back on the bus, a lively discussion broke out about the protagonist, Nora, who abandons her patronizing husband and their children. "She left the kids—I don't think that was right at all," said a girl named Nicole. "If you are a mother, you have to take care of the kids."

"I like the fact that she left the husband," Nancy said. "She saw that she had to be independent and that no girl needs to be tied up to a man, but I don't like the fact that she left her kids behind. If you abandon your kid, that is just like giving up on life."

A Shaky Support System

In the spring of 2010, Nancy heard from her mother, who was planning to illegally cross the border back into the United States in time for Nancy's June due date. Nancy was elated. But a few weeks later, she heard that her mother had been diagnosed with pelvic cancer and wouldn't be making the trip after all.

I found myself wondering what kind of support Nancy would have for the baby, especially once she had to leave McCabe. And so one afternoon I rode the school bus home with Nancy and joined her and her boyfriend, John, at a local pizzeria. John was slim and handsome, with gelled hair, a boyish face, and a trace of a mustache. They held hands nervously as Nancy recalled how they had met: "It was love at first sight. Everyone knew I liked him, except him."

Nancy said that her biggest source of frustration with John was how much time he spent playing video games like *Call of Duty*. "When he stops playing video games, he will pay more attention to me," she told me with a smile. She paused for a moment. "How old are guys when they stop playing video games?"

After finishing our pizza, we set off to meet Nancy's father, who lives in a small duplex overlooking a highway. The walls of the apartment were bare, as if the family had just moved in or perhaps was ready to move out at any time.

Nancy's father, a landscaper, looked exhausted. He told me that the prospect of supporting Nancy and Diana as well as his wife and their three children so troubled him that he sometimes couldn't sleep at night. "I worry, what if something happens and I die tomorrow?" he said, glancing at Nancy. "Who will help her?"

Nancy had the good fortune of being at school on the June afternoon she went into labor. She hurried to Bernadette Strode's office, and the principal called Nancy's father. "His response was, 'Well, just take her home,'" Strode recalls. "I said: 'No sir, that is not something I can do. She is going to have the baby today.' I decided I was going to override him. It was my call, and if he didn't like it, he could call my supervisor."

Strode drove Nancy to Yale-New Haven Hospital. Nancy's science teacher, Elizabeth Bradshaw, came along, too. "Nancy just kept saying, 'Thank you, thank you, thank you,'" Bradshaw says. Strode and Bradshaw helped get Nancy situated in a delivery room. John and his mother soon arrived, and later that day, Nancy gave birth to a healthy baby boy. She named him John.

Life Beyond McCabe

Just two weeks later, Nancy was back at McCabe to attend an end-of-the-year ceremony. Her newborn was wrapped in a light-blue blanket, and Nancy held him tight to her chest. I noticed that her face-piercing was gone and asked her about it. She said that, as a mother, she now felt such things were "inappropriate."

After a buffet lunch, teachers presented awards to the best and most improved students in each discipline. Nancy received awards for best student in English, art, history, biology, and life skills. She stole the show.

Baltimore's Laurence Paquin School for Pregnant and Parenting Teens Makes a Difference

I would have dropped out of my original school because I was embarrassed of being pregnant. I did not want anyone to look at me like I am another statistic, as a teenage mom, and I felt embarrassed about that. Here in the Paquin School, they encourage me to come to school every day. They make sure that I come to school. They call home, send letter if I do not come to school. Attendance is an important thing here. Here in the Paquin School, teachers give you individual attention. Before coming to the Paquin School, I was not good in Math. But I learned it after coming here, I am actually learning more here.

Ruhul Amin et al., "A Study of an Alternative School for Pregnant and/or Parenting Teens: Quantitative and Qualitative Evidence," Child and Adolescent Social Work Journal, *April 2006.*

But the ceremony also marked the end of Nancy's tenure at McCabe. The school's child-care program is small and designed to accommodate only infants up to the age of 3 months, and so she had to move on. In September, she started her junior year at Wilbur Cross, a public school in the East Rock section of New Haven, which has a day-care program for its teen mothers.

At her new school, Nancy now says, she sometimes feels overwhelmed. She says there are fights there, even among pregnant girls, and the teachers are so busy that they don't have time to talk with her the way the ones at McCabe did.

No matter how much Nancy may have benefited from her time at McCabe, I had assumed that the demands of motherhood were bound to limit her opportunities. Yet when researchers have compared the outcomes of pregnant teens with those of their closest peers—such as the girls' childless sisters or pregnant teens who have miscarried—findings show that childbearing itself worsens their outcomes only marginally or in the short term. According to the research, the most decisive factor in all of these young women's lives, whether they had children or not, is their disadvantaged backgrounds.

This seems to suggest that what Polly McCabe is really doing, more than anything else, is giving kids the tools they need to overcome the obstacles of poverty. And the lessons appear to be working for Nancy, who is now taking three honors classes and making plans to go to college.

Perhaps she is an example of what good can come when schools don't mainstream students with special needs; but her success may also simply indicate that any time a school system can afford to lavish attention on students who might otherwise be neglected, great things can happen.

At one point, Victoria Seitz, one of the researchers who studied McCabe students, asked me a question: "Why should only pregnant teens be able to get the kind of education offered at Polly McCabe?" It's a question, as it turns out, that Nancy's sister, Diana, has also asked.

On the day before Nancy started at Wilbur Cross, Strode stopped by her apartment to say hello. She asked Nancy how she planned on getting to school, and Nancy admitted that she didn't know. "OK," said Strode. "We need to straighten that out right now." She made several calls until she confirmed that Nancy would be picked up by a bus at 7:15 A.M. directly in front of her building. Strode then offered to help Nancy find a job and asked her to call if she ever needed anything. "You'll be fine," Strode said.

After Strode left, Diana turned to me. "I would like to get that kind of attention, too," she said.

> *"Fewer than 50 percent of the pregnancy school students successfully made a transition back to high school."*

Alternative Schools for Pregnant Teens Have Failed to Provide Adequate Education for Their Students

Julie Bosman

In the following viewpoint, Julie Bosman describes how many New York authorities are shutting down schools designed for pregnant teens. According to Bosman, city and school officials recognize that separate schools both segregate these teens from their peers and do little to improve their educational outcomes. She relates stories of ineffectual classroom instruction and distractions that keep girls from focusing on learning. In addition, Bosman notes that pregnant teens may have plans of furthering their studies, but statistics show that many struggle with academic performance and eventually drop out of alternative programs. For these reasons, cities are rethinking the value of pregnancy schools. Bosman is a reporter for the New York Times.

A dozen girls, some perched awkwardly with their pregnant bellies flush against the desks, were struggling over a high school geometry assignment on a recent afternoon.

No pencils, no textbooks, no Pythagorean theorem. Instead, they sewed quilts.

That is what passes for math in one of New York City's four high schools for pregnant girls, this one in Harlem. "It ties into geometry," said Patricia Martin, the principal. "They're cutting shapes."

Created in the 1960s, when pregnant girls were such pariahs that they were forced to leave school until their babies were born, the city school system's four pregnancy schools—or P-schools, as they are obliquely referred to—have lived on, their population dwindling to just 323 students from 1,500 in the late 1960s.

They have been marked by abysmal test scores, poor attendance and inadequate facilities, and even some of their own administrators say they suspect that most of their students are pushed there by other schools because they are failing academically. In place of proms and computer labs, they have Mother's Day parties and day care centers with cribs lining the walls.

The Demise of P-Schools

Now in recognition of their failure, the city plans to shut them down at the end of the school year as part of a sweeping reorganization to be announced today [May 24, 2007] of the alternative school district, which also includes an array of vocational, technical and dropout programs for students who have struggled in traditional settings.

"It's a separate but unequal program," acknowledges Cami Anderson, the superintendent whose district includes the Program for Pregnant Students, as it is formally called. "The girls get pushed out of their original high schools, they don't come to class and they don't gain ground in terms of credits."

The Limited Offerings in Alternative Schools for Pregnant and Parenting Teens

Beyond a few stats on the [California] Department of Education's website, it's tough to track students' academic success at alternative schools. They aren't rated on the state's Academic Performance Index, the main statewide accountability system.

Defenders of continuation schools insist that they offer a comparable (just different) way of teaching the same curriculum. But that's not entirely true.

"We cannot do physics or chemistry. [Broadway High School in San Jose is] too small . . . to offer the array," principal Kathy Wein says. "There are lots of school districts who don't offer all that." She adds that it may take longer to head down a career path via Broadway, but students will get there. "You're not crippled. This is not a dead end to anything that you want."

Allie Gottlieb, "You Can't Come to School,"
Metro (San Jose, CA), April 10, 2003.

The schools' demise, like their origins, may be a sign of changing times. Pregnancy schools across the country appear to be slowly fading away, partly stemming from the decade-long declining rate of teenage pregnancy and partly because of the idea that the girls should not be segregated from other students. These days, nearly 40 New York City high schools have their own day care centers.

The number of pregnancy schools in Chicago has dwindled to one. In Madison, Wis., enrollment in pregnancy schools has decreased by roughly 15 percent over the last five years, said Ken Syke, a spokesman for the public schools there. And in the Los Angeles public schools, the teaching staff at one pregnancy school has dropped to 16 from 19 in three years, and shut down one of its five sites.

"They have definitely trended down in population from five years ago," said Ken Easum, the administrative coordinator of Educational Options, the alternative public schools program in Los Angeles.

In New York, the girls in the Program for Pregnant Students make up only a small portion of the 7,000 girls enrolled in the city's public schools who become pregnant each year, according to city health department estimates.

Segregating Pregnant Teens

The decision to close the schools came after a six-month study commissioned by the Education Department essentially concluded that the girls, eager to earn high school diplomas despite their pregnancies, had been relegated to a second-class tier of schools that treat them more like mothers-to-be than curious students.

For years, too, a range of groups had railed against the schools as vestiges of an almost Victorian past, arguing that they were sexist, stigmatizing and demeaning, and that the majority of the students who leave the one-year program were even further behind academically than before their pregnancies.

"It is a place that they send young women during their pregnancies, and I can't think of any sound academic reason that they exist," said Benita Miller, the executive director of the Brooklyn Young Mothers' Collective, a nonprofit group that holds monthly workshops in the schools.

Before the schools were established in the 1960s, pregnant girls were put on "medical suspension" until after their babies were born, then banned from returning to their original high schools afterward. Hundreds of other girls were sent, often under threat of court order, to shelters, where the old Board of Education maintained special schools.

But many of the girls remained unaware of their educational rights. In 1970, the New York Civil Liberties Union published a handbook outlining the rights of New York City public school students. One of those rights, it said, was "to remain in your regular school program as long as physically possible" while pregnant.

Title IX of the Education Amendments of 1972 stated that schools were allowed to create separate educational programs for pregnant students, but that they must be of comparable quality to standard high schools.

Mainstream High Schools Routinely Push Pregnant Teens Out

Ms. Anderson, the superintendent who was installed 10 months ago [as of 2007], said that many students in the pregnancy schools had not been thriving in their regular high schools.

Some school administrators and students say that guidance counselors, eager to push out struggling students in an era in which poor performance can carry sanctions, routinely strongarm newly pregnant girls to drop out and enroll in a pregnancy school.

Dannette Queen, the assistant principal at the pregnancy school in Harlem, said most students were referred by a guidance counselor. "The pregnancies provide the guidance counselors the perfect opportunity to get rid of them and say, 'You need to be in a pregnant school,'" Ms. Queen said. "Some guidance counselors tell them they won't have to go to class when they come here."

Still, some girls currently enrolled in pregnancy schools rhapsodize about their desire to get a high school diploma, go to college and pursue careers. Kyasia Davis, a tall, bubbly 18-year-old who is enrolled in the pregnancy school in the Bronx, says she wants to attend community college after she graduates.

Sitting in a science classroom at the pregnancy school in Harlem, Cassandra Gonzalez, 15, who is expecting a boy in July, says she plans to go to college and become a lawyer. But the constant talk of babies at school, she adds, often distracts from studying.

Some cities are rethinking the value of special schools for pregnant teens and feel the teens would be more successful if they were integrated into regular schools. © Jon Riley/The Image Bank/Getty Images.

"Sometimes, you have girls who come in with their babies," she said. "Then it's like, forget class!"

Some teachers and administrators who have worked in the schools for years believe in them and say they were designed with students' safety and well-being in mind. In regular high schools, many girls feel ostracized by other students, they say, and struggle to keep up once they are distracted by the burdens of pregnancy.

"It's a necessary thing for those students who can't succeed in a regular high school setting," said Eleanor McDonagh, the assistant principal at the pregnancy school in Brooklyn.

Pregnant Teens Often Drop Out of School

But teachers say many girls, disillusioned with the pregnancy schools, do not last long there either. In a class meant to teach child-rearing skills at the Bronx school, a room of only a half-dozen girls listlessly sewed pillows for their babies' cribs. Barbara

Haughton, the teacher, said the low attendance was unusual. "Many of them are on maternity leave," she said. The students are allowed two months of leave after they give birth and cannot bring their babies to the school day care center until they are 2 months old.

Another teacher at the Brooklyn school, Linda Lloyd-Jones, said she had seen girls, juggling classes with impending motherhood, abandon high school out of frustration. "A lot of them leave right after the first semester because they can't stand it," Ms. Lloyd-Jones said.

The internal data provided to the Education Department by a private consultant showed what dismal results the pregnancy schools have yielded. In the fall of 2006, the average daily attendance at the pregnancy schools was 47 percent, well below the city average. Fewer than 50 percent of the pregnancy school students successfully made a transition back to high school. And the average student only earned four to five credits each year, fewer than half of the 11 credits possible.

It's not for lack of spending: the Education Department spent $33,670 on each student this year, a cost of more than $10.8 million—more than double the citywide average of per-pupil spending. Ms. Anderson, the superintendent, said she hoped that starting next year, pregnant girls would remain in their regular high schools or switch to small specialized high schools designed for struggling students. "The most powerful thing we can do for parenting teens is help them get their diplomas," she said. "Your brain does not die when you become pregnant."

| "*A parenting course can greatly increase the success rate of our future families.*"

High Schools Should Implement Parenting Classes for All Students

Teresa Armstrong

In the following viewpoint, Teresa Armstrong argues that high schools should require parenting classes for students. In her view, such courses would teach young people about pregnancy and parenting, making them more responsible as they move toward adulthood. Armstrong also contends that parenting classes would help lower the number of unwanted pregnancies and thus serve in part as a remedy to the problem of overpopulation. Armstrong is a writer who has contributed to the informational website Helium.

Parenting class should be a mandatory subject [for] all high school students [who] must attend and complete with a passing grade in order to graduate. A parenting course can reduce unwanted pregnancy, lower over population, and prepare for families. Parenting is an expected and anticipated part of human

Some argue that mandatory pregnancy and parenting classes in high schools could help reduce unwanted teen pregnancies. © AP Photo/The Indianapolis Star/Michelle Pemberton.

nature. Children are brought [up] to want a family and long for the attention of family members whether it be parents or siblings. Informing young adults of the pro[s] and cons of parenting would contribute to how and when [they] begin . . . a family.

Reducing Unwanted Pregnancy

First, reducing unwanted pregnancy is a factor we must get under control. A parenting class would give young adults the chance to learn what happens to these unwanted babies, whether they are put up for adoption, aborted, or abused. There are numerous children put up for adoption. Adoption is wonderful for some adults; however, not all children can be adopted and therefore [many] live in foster homes or places that are not always suitable even for animals. Abortion is always an option. Abortion is not the most reasonable considering there are ways of preventing the murder of unborn children. Abortion is also expensive; nevertheless, this is an option for many young adults that would rather

Implementing Parenting Education Courses for Students

Effective childrearing takes knowledge, education, and economic resources. A national family policy could direct national resources toward providing the support needed for effective parenting. Also, an in-school mandatory education for parenthood, with a strong child development component, could be helpful in developing parenting skills. . . .

Ample material and course outlines are available for the implementation of parenting courses. Such materials can be introduced at many levels, for example, as a course in home economics (but for both sexes); as a part of a social studies course examining the study of family roles and responsibilities; as part of the study of civics, examining the American promise of the rights of life, liberty, and the pursuit of happiness. Further such courses can be implemented in the elementary school, in junior high school, or in high schools.

Nicholas Anastasiow, "Should Parenting Education Be Mandatory?," Topics in Early Childhood Special Education, *February 1988.*

keep the pregnancy a secret. Some young adults are brought up with different morals or beliefs, and these two alternatives are not always an option; therefore, many unwanted children become abused or neglected children.

Keeping Population Growth in Check

Second, lower population in the U.S is always an issue. Parenting class can reduce the amount of pregnancy. Supplying the knowledge . . . needed for preventing pregnancy can greatly lower our already overpopulated society, thus creating more money for scholarships, grants, and unused money to further the education of these young adults. This also increases the jobs for our educated young people without the restrictions and obstacles created by having babies at an early age.

Preparing Young People for Parenting

Third, a parenting course can greatly increase the success rate of our future families. By preparing young adults on the aspects of raising a family we can greatly reduce the divorce rate that continues to increase. Preparing young women for the duties of being a housewife or parent lowers the unexpected expectations that many young women are unaware of. Television, radio, and the Internet contribute to the often illusionary way of life. Many young adults are not aware of the day in and day out responsibilities of [raising] a family or [being] a parent.

Parenting class at high schools should be mandatory in the preparation of our young adult lives. While lowering unwanted pregnancy, lowering over population, and preparing for family [are] wonderful tools needed for these students, we also teach them responsibility. Knowledge is key to success, and most young adults start with knowledge from their own family life. Let's continue to grow with successful families and educated young adults by making parenting a required course of all high school students.

"Are we making it easier for girls to make a bad choice and helping them avoid the truth about the consequences?"

Government Welfare and School Assistance Programs May Be Encouraging Teen Pregnancy

Patrick Welsh

In the following viewpoint, Patrick Welsh takes issue with the public support system for pregnant teens. Welsh criticizes the culture in which many girls are becoming pregnant without shame or fear of hardship. He believes that schools and the government are encouraging teen pregnancy by providing a safety net that assists young mothers without judging their actions. Although Welsh acknowledges that these parents need help, he worries that both schools and welfare programs are ignoring the problem of teen pregnancy in the rush to provide services. Welsh contends that communities and social services should focus on imparting the financial, educational, and social trials of teen pregnancy to enlighten young people about the consequences of the choices they make. Welsh is a teacher at T.C. Williams High School in Alexandria, Virginia.

The girls gather in small groups outside Alexandria's [Virginia] T.C. Williams High School most mornings, standing with their babies on their hips, talking and giggling like sorority sisters. Sometimes their mothers drop the kids (and their kids) off with a carefree smile and a wave. As I watch the girls carry their children into the Tiny Titans day-care center in our new $100 million building, I can't help wondering what Sister Mary Avelina, my 11th-grade English teacher, would have thought.

A Troubling Picture

Okay, I'm an old guy from the 1950s, an era light-years from today. But even in these less censorious times, I'm amazed—and concerned—by the apparently nonchalant attitude both these girls and their mothers exhibit in front of teachers, administrators and hundreds of students each day. Last I heard, teen pregnancy is still a major concern in this country—teenage mothers are less likely to finish school and more likely to live in poverty; their children are more likely to have difficulties in school and with the law; and on and on.

But none of that seems to register with these young women. In fact, "some girls seem to be really into it," says T.C. senior Mary Ball. "They are embracing their pregnancies." Nor is the sight of a pregnant classmate much of a surprise to the students at T.C. anymore. "When I was in middle school, I'd be shocked to see a pregnant eighth-grader," says Ball. "Now it seems so ordinary that we don't even talk about it."

Teenage pregnancy has been bright on American radar screens for the past year: TV teen starlet Jamie Lynn Spears's pregnancy caused a minor media storm last December [2007]. The pregnant-teen movie "Juno" won Oscar nods. And there was Bristol Palin, daughter of Alaska Gov. Sarah Palin, bringing the issue front and center during the recent presidential campaign. But I've been observing the phenomenon up close for a couple of years now, and the picture I see is more troubling than any of those high-profile pregnancies make it seem.

Government Funding for Sexual Education Programs Sends the Wrong Message to Teens

Early sexual activity has harmful effects on the health, psychological well-being, and long-term life prospects of teens, and these harmful effects will be reduced only slightly by contraceptive use.

Regrettably, relatively few teens receive a clear message about the harmful effects of early sexual activity; few are taught that society expects teens to delay sexual activity. Instead, most safe sex/ comprehensive sex-ed programs send the clear, if implicit, message that society expects and condones teen sexual activity. The main message is that it's okay for teens to have sex as long as they use condoms.

Melissa G. Pardue, Robert E. Rector, and Shannan Martin, "Government Spends $12 on Safe Sex and Contraceptives for Every $1 Spent on Abstinence," Heritage Foundation Backgrounder No. 1718, January 14, 2004.

Ignoring Personal Responsibility in the Rush to Assist Teen Mothers

The somber statistics about teen motherhood are the reason the day-care center, run by the local nonprofit Campagna Center, was opened in T.C. Williams two years ago. The idea is to keep the girls in school, let them get their diplomas and help them avoid the kind of fate described earlier. I've been a teacher for more than 30 years, and I want the best for my students and to help them succeed in every way possible. I know that these girls need support. But I can't help thinking we're going at this all wrong.

On the surface, Alexandria seems to be striving to stem teen pregnancy. Every high school student is required to take a "family life" course that teaches about birth control, sexually transmitted disease and teen pregnancy. The Adolescent Health Center, a clinic providing birth control, was built a few blocks from the school. The city-run Campaign on Adolescent Pregnancy sponsors workshops for parents and teens. But none of this coalesces to hit the teens with the message that getting pregnant is a disaster. And within the school, apart from the family life class, the attitude is laissez-faire, as if teachers and administrators are afraid to address the issue for fear of offending the students who have children.

Once a girl gets pregnant, though, the school leaps in to do everything for her. But I wonder: Is it possible that all this assistance—with little or no comment about the kids' actions— has the unintended effect of actually encouraging them to get pregnant? Are we making it easier for girls to make a bad choice and helping them avoid the truth about the consequences?

And for many, it does seem to be a choice. "There's a myth that these pregnancies are accidental," says school nurse Nancy Runton. "But many of them aren't. I've known girls who've made 'I'll get pregnant if you get pregnant' pacts. It's a status thing. These girls go around school telling each other how beautiful they look pregnant, how cute their tummies look."

Pregnancy pacts, too, were in the news earlier this year when a group of girls in a Massachusetts high school reportedly made one (though some denied it). But that's only one way the situation at T.C. reflects what's happening across the country. The birth rate among teens, after falling 36 percent since 1990, went up 3 percent in 2006, the first increase in 15 years. And most of the rise is due to pregnancies among Hispanic girls.

Living in a No-Shame Dream World

Lots of white teens nationally have babies, but that's not really the case at T.C. Teen motherhood here is mostly a class issue— and given Alexandria's demographics, that means the teen mothers are virtually all lower-income blacks and Hispanics with few financial or other resources. Moreover, the number of Hispanic girls with babies is double the number of black girls, which also reflects a national trend. According to Sarah Brown, director of the National Campaign to Prevent Teen and Unplanned Pregnancy, Hispanics now have the highest rate of teen pregnancy and births of any racial or ethnic group in the country.

In our school of 2,211 students, we now have at least 70 girls who are soon-to-be or already mothers. Many T.C. teachers and administrators have decidedly mixed emotions about the situation. Social worker Terri Wright says that for many girls, getting pregnant before they turn 18 is a rite of passage. "They don't wear sweatshirts or baggy dresses to conceal their pregnancies," says Wright. "I get invitations to baby showers. Girls bring me pictures of their kids dressed up like little dolls."

"There is zero shame," agrees school nurse Runton. One girl walked into a colleague's class last month, announced that she was pregnant and began showing her sonogram around. Another 16-year-old proudly proclaimed that she was "going on maternity leave." The teacher tried to explain that maternity leave is a job benefit that doesn't apply to high school students.

"I don't personally accept it, but once a girl is pregnant, I have to be all open arms," Wright says.

The pregnant teens' classmates don't necessarily applaud the phenomenon, either. "These girls having babies are living in a dream world," says Lauren Heming, a senior in my AP English class. "They think that because the school is giving them all this help now, things will be easy for them when they graduate." Kayla Tall, another senior, sees lots of girls as under "great pressure to grow up fast by having sex." And, she says, "A lot of girls think that if they have the baby, they can keep hanging on to the boyfriend. In fact, these guys are little boys who have used the girls to prove themselves to each other."

The Trials of Teen Parenting

I'd be less than honest if I didn't admit that I'm torn about T.C.'s teen moms and the Tiny Titans center. As upset as I get at the

School health centers that provide birth control, such as this one in Portland, Maine, have been criticized by some as encouraging sexual behavior in teens. © AP Photo/Cheryl Senter.

recklessness I see in some of the girls and their boyfriends, I can't begrudge someone like Cynthia Quinteros the help she needs to raise her one-year-old son. "If it wasn't for the day-care center, I would have to quit school to take care of Angel," says the 16-year-old. "My mother is a single mom, and my brother is 11. My mom has to work."

Cynthia's days are grueling. She gets up at 6 A.M., feeds and dresses Angel and is at school by 7:50. She drops Angel off at the center, eats breakfast in the cafeteria and heads for class. Her mom picks her and the baby up at 3:15 P.M. At home, Cynthia eats, plays with Angel, starts homework and then leaves at 4:50 for her supermarket cashier's job. She gets home at 10:10, does a little homework and goes to bed.

Cynthia says that lots of her friends actively tried to get pregnant, but she didn't. Like many girls she knows, she was getting a shot of the contraceptive DMPA/Depo-Provera every three months at the teen health clinic starting when she was 13. (Which evokes further conflicting emotions on my part and surely must do the same to health-care providers called upon to provide birth-control shots to 13-year-old girls.)

Cynthia would tell her mom that she had to stay after school and then go to the clinic, but when her mother insisted that she come home right away, she missed her shots and got pregnant at 15 by an 18-year-old guy. She says that all her friends who have babies wish they had waited. "They've learned the hard way," she says. "None of them want to have another baby now. Most of them are getting their Depo shots regularly."

Angel's father isn't involved with the baby, but not all the guys who father children by teenage girls are AWOL. Every morning, 19-year-old Gustavo Martinez drives 16-year-old Karla Becerra to school and carries their 3-month-old son into day care before going to work for a local contractor. He's at school by 4 every day to pick them up. "My father was never around, and I don't want to have that happen to my son," Gustavo told me. He says he's saving money so that he and Karla can have their own place and get married.

A Widespread Problem Supported by Welfare

But they are very much the exception. The fact is, says Robert Wolverton, medical director of the teen health clinic, most of these girls and their families see no problem with being unmarried and having a child at 16 or 17.

According to the Virginia Department of Health, there were 204 pregnancies among Alexandria teens in 2006, resulting in 102 births and 99 abortions. Pregnancy rates among Latinas were the highest of any group.

The Tiny Titans center is at maximum capacity and has a long waiting list. It currently cares for eight babies ranging from 6 weeks to 24 months, eight toddlers from 24 months to 36 months and 18 children from 3 to 5 years of age.

Most of the mothers are in free and reduced school-lunch programs, and few have insurance. So when they get pregnant, a whole tax-supported industry kicks into action: The Health Department assigns a nurse to the girl, a group called Resource Mothers is notified to pick girls up at school or home and drive them to doctor's appointments, and the Campagna Center plans day care for the child. The school dietitian plans nutritious meals for the mothers. The federally funded WIC [Women, Infants, and Children] program provides free formula, milk, cheese, peanut butter and the like to the teens and their babies. In Virginia, girls from 13 on up are eligible for free reproductive services—prenatal care, hospital visits and delivery.

According to a study by the National Campaign to Prevent Teen and Unplanned Pregnancy, teen childbearing nationwide cost taxpayers $9.1 billion in 2004. Teens 17 and under—the ages of most of the girls at T.C.—account for $8.6 billion of that total, or an average of $4,080 per teen mother annually.

School social worker David Wynne states the obvious: "Whatever we're doing, it's not working." It's hard to say whether other school districts do any better than Alexandria at discouraging teen pregnancy. According to Brown, school sex-ed programs nationwide are a patchwork that includes everything from required HIV/AIDS education to using students as peer counselors to abstinence-only programs. No one really knows what's working where. But at T.C., I know that almost every adult involved in helping our girls seems to be at a loss, especially in the face of the rising birth rate among Hispanics.

Cynthia Quinteros, however, has a theory. "I feel that the community is afraid to talk about all the girls who are getting pregnant," she says. "Once you get pregnant, they do everything for you, but they ought to be doing all they can do to show girls how difficult their lives will be if they have a baby. I love Angel, but if I didn't have him I wouldn't have to work after school, I could study more, I could be a normal teenager."

Out of the mouths of babes.

15

> "Welfare removes some of the negative economic consequences of out-of-wedlock births, and thus encourages more such births."

Temporary Assistance to Needy Families (TANF) Should Be Terminated

Michael Tanner and Tad DeHaven

In the following viewpoint, Michael Tanner and Tad DeHaven argue that government assistance to needy families is ineffective and should be terminated. According to the authors, welfare creates a culture of dependence that discourages recipients from looking for work, and this cycle repeats through generations of welfare families. Tanner and DeHaven contend that the 1996 reform laws set limits on how long recipients could draw aid and established Temporary Assistance to Needy Families (TANF) as a block grant to help states provide for the poor. However, Tanner and DeHaven maintain that states have taken advantage of loopholes and exceptions in TANF that allow them to continue assistance beyond preset limits, undoing the notion of "temporary assistance." In addition, the authors believe the extension of welfare programs and the value of the payments have encouraged young girls to bear chil-

Michael Tanner and Tad DeHaven, "TANF and Federal Welfare," *Cato Institute: Downsizing the Federal Government*, September 2010. Copyright © 2010 Cato Institute. All rights reserved. Reproduced by permission.

dren out of wedlock because they are confident that a government safety net is in place to take care of them. Tanner and DeHaven claim that the system needs to be scrapped so that private charities can step in to provide more focused aid to those in need. Tanner is a senior fellow at the Cato Institute, a libertarian public policy organization. DeHaven is an analyst on federal and state budget issues for the Cato Institute.

The federal government funds a large range of subsidy programs for low-income Americans, from food stamps to Medicaid. This [viewpoint] examines Temporary Assistance for Needy Families (TANF), which is a joint federal-state cash assistance program for low-income families with children. When most people think of "welfare," they are thinking of this program.

Since a major welfare reform in 1996, federal spending on TANF has been held fairly constant at somewhat less than $20 billion per year. The 2009 American Recovery and Reinvestment Act provided an additional $5 billion in federal funding over several years. About 1.8 million families receive TANF payments each month.

Before 1996, federal welfare was an open-ended entitlement that encouraged long-term dependency, and there was widespread agreement that it was a terrible failure. It neither reduced poverty nor helped the poor become self-sufficient. It encouraged out-of-wedlock births and weakened the work ethic. The pathologies it engendered were passed from generation to generation.

The welfare reforms of 1996 were dramatic, but the federal government still runs an array of welfare programs that are expensive and damaging. The federal government should phaseout its role in TANF and related welfare programs and leave low-income assistance programs to state governments, or better yet, the private sector.

Government welfare cannot provide the same flexibility and diversity as private charities. Private aid organizations have a better understanding that true charity starts with individuals making better life choices. Federal involvement in welfare has generated an expensive mess of paperwork and bureaucracy while doing little to solve the problem of long-term poverty.

A Brief History of Federal Welfare

The first federal welfare program was Aid to Dependent Children (ADC), which was created as part of President Franklin Roosevelt's New Deal in 1935. The program was intended to supplement existing state relief programs for widows and to provide support to families in which the father was deceased, absent, or unable to work.

Although it was originally supposed to be a small program, ADC expanded rapidly. By 1938, almost 250,000 families were participating in the program. Despite rapid economic growth and declining levels of poverty during the 1950s, ADC rolls continued to grow. By 1956, over 600,000 families were receiving benefits.

In 1960, President John F. Kennedy took office amidst rising concern about poverty in America. But beyond renaming ADC to Aid to Families with Dependent Children (AFDC) and expanding it to include two-parent families in which the father was unemployed, Kennedy actually took little action on welfare. But Kennedy's general support for expanding aid to the poor set the stage for Lyndon Johnson's Great Society.

After Kennedy's assassination [on November 22, 1963], Johnson had a free hand in Congress, and he was determined to use it to remake government and society. Johnson declared that the federal government would wage a War on Poverty and his administration proposed a huge array of new subsidy programs for individuals and state and local governments. America had not seen such an expansion of government or such a proliferation of anti-poverty programs since the New Deal. Among the major Johnson initiatives were Medicare, Medicaid, and Head Start.

The proliferation of new urban programs, job training, health care, and other welfare activities during the 1960s coincided with further expansions in AFDC. By 1965 the number of people receiving AFDC had risen to 4.3 million. By 1972 the number had more than doubled to nearly 10 million. The welfare rolls were rapidly expanding even though this was a period of general economic prosperity and low unemployment.

After Johnson left office, there was a bipartisan consensus in Washington to preserve and even expand his legacy. Presidents Nixon, Ford, and Carter all added new anti-poverty programs. Between 1965 and 1975, measured in constant dollars, spending for AFDC tripled. A series of court decisions that established "rights" for welfare recipients helped fuel the spending growth. After 1975, the growth rate of welfare slowed but still continued upward.

In 1981, President Ronald Reagan came into office with strong views about shrinking the welfare state. Unfortunately, welfare-related spending actually grew during Reagan's two terms. Reagan did shift the funding emphasis among welfare-related programs. For example, funding for AFDC declined by 1 percent during his tenure, but spending for the Earned Income Tax Credit doubled.

By the time President Bill Clinton took office in 1993, a broad national consensus had developed that traditional open-ended welfare had failed. This led to a period of state-government experimentation with welfare within the constraints that the federal government allowed them. Many state experiments—particularly work requirements and recipient time limits—would become part of federal welfare reform in 1996.

Welfare Reform in 1996

In August 1996, President Clinton signed into law the Personal Responsibility and Work Opportunity Reconciliation Act (PRWORA), which represented the most extensive revision of federal welfare in more than 30 years. By one important measure, welfare reform was very successful. The number of Americans on welfare plunged from 12.6 million in 1996 to 4.2 million individuals by 2009, a dramatic 67-percent decrease.

The reform bill made a number of significant changes in the way welfare was provided. AFDC had provided cash payments to families with children where the parents were absent, incapacitated, deceased, or unemployed. The program was funded by a combination of federal and state funds (the federal portion varied from 50 to 80 percent), with states setting benefit levels and the federal government determining eligibility requirements. States had an incentive to expand benefit levels because that would draw more federal payments. And recipients could stay on the program for years on end.

PRWORA replaced AFDC with the Temporary Assistance for Needy Families block grant. The block grant was a fixed amount of federal funds for each state, largely based on the pre-reform federal contribution to that state's AFDC program. However, this caused states that had offered more generous welfare benefits to receive much more federal money per poor family than other states received.

Welfare reform in 1996 abolished most federal eligibility and payment rules, giving states much greater flexibility to design their own programs. The reforms eliminated welfare's "entitlement" status so that no one would have an automatic right to benefits. States could choose which families to help. States were, however, required to continue spending at least 80 percent of their previous levels under a "maintenance of effort" provision.

In recent years, federal spending on TANF has been held fairly constant at somewhat less than $20 billion per year. Combined federal and state TANF spending was about $26 billion in 2006. About 41 percent was for direct cash assistance, with the remainder of the subsidies for childcare, transportation, work support, and education and training. Administrative costs accounted for almost 10 percent of expenditures.

That represents a significant change in the distribution of expenditures from pre-reform welfare. Prior to reform, cash assistance accounted for 73 percent of welfare spending under AFDC and related programs.

Some argue that private charities, such as food banks, may be a better alternative than government-funded programs to provide assistance to low-income families. © Spencer Platt/ Getty Images.

Under the old AFDC system, many welfare recipients seemed trapped in almost permanent dependency on government aid. To combat this, welfare reform established time limits to prevent welfare from becoming a way of life. PRWORA set a federal limit of five years, but allowed states to set shorter time limits if they wished.

While this sounds fairly strict, it was undercut somewhat because states were allowed to exempt up to 20 percent of their caseloads from time limits, and were also allowed to use their own funds to continue benefits for families that exceeded the federal five-year time limit. In addition, so-called "children only" cases, where the child is eligible for welfare benefits, but the adult parent is not, are not subject to federal time limits. Children-only cases account for almost half of the total TANF caseload.

Work Requirements Fail to Make Significant Impact

The 1996 welfare reform imposed widespread work requirements on recipients. States are required to have at least 50 percent of eligible welfare recipients from single parent families participating in work activities. For two-parent families, the participation requirement is 90 percent. As of 2006, every state except Indiana had technically met the mandate for all families.

However, states were given various credits and exemptions that significantly reduced the number of recipients required to work. For example, states receive a credit based on their caseload reductions. Because welfare rolls have plummeted, the average effective minimum work participation requirement in 2006 was only 5.0 percent for all families and 18.7 percent for two-parent families. In fact, for 17 states and two territories, the credit has reduced the effective work requirement to *zero,* and only 21 states have an effective minimum greater than 10 percent. Thus, nearly all the states have carved out large exemptions from their work requirements.

After all the credits, waivers, and exemptions are taken into account, only 32 percent of welfare recipients were working in 2009. While this is low, it does represent a substantial improvement over pre-reform welfare. Under the old AFDC program, only about 10 percent of recipients were working.

Note that just because a recipient is participating in "work activities" under today's welfare does not mean that the individual is actually working. For example, in almost all states, simply looking for work constitutes a "work activity," which allows people to continue receiving their welfare check.

The work component of welfare reform was a big step in the right direction, but the actual changes to work behavior have been modest. Because of exemptions built into the 1996 law, most states are not really required to make a large number of recipients work, and few states have chosen to do so on their own.

Welfare Linked to a Rise in Out-of-Wedlock Childbearing

The tragedy of government welfare programs is not just wasted taxpayer money but wasted lives. The effects of welfare in encouraging the break-up of low-income families have been extensively documented. The primary way that those with low incomes can advance in the market economy is to get married, stay married, and work—but welfare programs have created incentives to do the opposite.

The number of single-parent families has risen dramatically since the 1960s. The most important reason for the rise in single-parent families is births to unmarried women. In 1965, less than 8 percent of all births were out of wedlock. Today the figure is 39 percent.

The policy concern about the increase in out-of-wedlock births is not a question of private morality. The concern is that out-of-wedlock childbearing remains overwhelmingly concentrated at the lowest rungs of the socio-economic ladder. Having a child out of wedlock at an early age for someone without career skills can mean a lifetime of poverty.

Of more than 20 major studies of the issue, more than three-quarters show a significant link between welfare benefit levels and out-of-wedlock childbearing. Higher benefit levels mean higher out-of-wedlock births. Children living with single mothers are seven times more likely to be poor than those living with two parents.

Welfare removes some of the negative economic consequences of out-of-wedlock births, and thus encourages more such births. More than 20 percent of single-mothers start on welfare because they have an out-of-wedlock birth, and 75 percent of government aid to children through means-tested programs like TANF goes to single-parent families. Moreover, once on welfare, single mothers find it difficult to get off, and they tend to stay on welfare for longer periods than other recipients.

Welfare's Negative Impact on Marriage Among Pregnant and Parenting Teens

Current tax and welfare policies also contain numerous disincentives for marriage. In our interviews, some White teen mothers told us that they are delaying marriage until they complete their vocational education, which for many young mothers would be impossible without means—tested state subsidies to cover tuition, medical care, and child care costs—subsidies for which they might well become ineligible were they to marry an employable man.

Some research also suggests that, while welfare benefits may not affect the likelihood that a single female will become pregnant, they do reduce the likelihood a single pregnant woman will marry the father of her child. One study also finds that receipt of welfare permanently reduces the likelihood an unwed mother will ever marry, even though there is no evidence that welfare recipients, compared to other women, have less desire for marriage. In short, some poor and working-class couples may be substituting informal unions for legal marriages at least partly in order to maintain family income.

Maggie Gallagher, The Age of Unwed Mothers: Is Teen Pregnancy the Problem? *New York: Institute for American Values, 1999.*

Focusing solely on the out-of-wedlock birthrate may actually understate the problem. In the past, women who gave birth out of wedlock frequently married the fathers of their children after the birth. As many as 85 percent of unwed mothers, in the 1950s, ultimately married the fathers of their children. Therefore, while technically born out of wedlock, the children were still likely to grow up in intact two-parent families.

However, the increasing availability and value of welfare have made such marriages less attractive for unwed mothers. If the father is unskilled and has poor employment prospects, a welfare check may seem a preferable alternative. Studies indicate that young mothers and pregnant women are less likely to marry the fathers of their children in states with higher welfare benefits. Nonetheless, 70 percent of poor single mothers would no longer be in poverty if they married their children's father.

Welfare is also likely to entrap the next generation as well. The attitudes and habits that lead to welfare dependency are transmitted the same way as other parent-to-child pathologies, such as alcoholism and child abuse. Although it is true that the majority of children raised on welfare will not receive welfare themselves, the rate of welfare dependence for children raised on it is far higher than for their non-welfare counterparts.

Children raised on welfare are likely to have lower incomes as adults than children not raised on welfare. The more welfare received by a child's family, the lower that child's earnings as an adult tend to be, even holding constant such other factors as race, family structure, and education. According to one study, nearly 20 percent of daughters from families that were "highly dependent" on welfare became "highly dependent" themselves, whereas only 3 percent of daughters from non-welfare households became "highly dependent" on welfare.

Welfare Provides a Disincentive to Work

The choice of welfare over work is often a rational decision based on economic incentives. Empirical studies confirm that welfare is a disincentive for work. For example, an analysis of interstate variation in labor force participation by economists Richard Vedder, Lowell Gallaway, and Robert Lawson found that such participation declined as welfare benefits increased. Similarly, Robert Moffitt of Brown University found that the work effort of welfare recipients was reduced by as much as 30 percent.

Such studies may understate the work disincentive of welfare because they consider only a small portion of the total package of federal and state welfare benefits. Benefits available to people in the welfare system that are not available to the working poor create an incentive to go on welfare and remain in the program once enrolled. For example, one study shows that education and training programs available under TANF may induce people to go on welfare.

Perhaps most troubling of all is the psychological attitude toward work that can develop among those on welfare. Studies have found that the poor on welfare do not have a strong sense that they need to take charge of their own lives or find work to become self-sufficient. Indeed, they often have a feeling that the government has an obligation to provide for them.

Of course, these psychological effects are also true for other government subsidy recipients, including farmers, the elderly, and businesses that are hooked on federal hand-outs of one sort or another. Farmers that are major subsidy recipients, for example, are less likely to make tough decisions to cut costs or diversify their income sources because they know they will be bailed out if market conditions sour on them. It is not healthy for any group in society to depend on government welfare for their long-term survival, whether they are farmers or poor inner-city families.

The Relationship Between Welfare and Crime

Children from single-parent families are more likely to become involved in criminal activity. Research indicates a direct cor-relation between crime rates and the number of single-parent families in a neighborhood. As welfare contributes to the rise in out-of-wedlock births, it thus also contributes to higher levels of criminal activity.

A Maryland National Association for the Advancement of Colored People (NAACP) report concluded that "the ready ac-cess to a lifetime of welfare and free social service programs is a major contributory factor to the crime problems we face today."

The NAACP's conclusion is confirmed by additional academic research. For example, research by M. Anne Hill and June O'Neill shows that a 50-percent increase in welfare and food stamp benefits led to a 117-percent increase in the crime rate among young black men.

Barbara Whitehead noted in an [April 1993] article in the *Atlantic Monthly*:

> The relationship [between single-parent families and crime] is so strong that controlling for family configuration erases the relationship between race and crime and between low income and crime. This conclusion shows up time and again in the literature. The nation's mayors, as well as police officers, social workers, probation officers, and court officials, consistently point to family breakup as the most important source of rising rates of crime.

Welfare leads to increased crime by contributing to the marginalization of young men in society. As author George Gilder noted, "The welfare culture tells the man he is not a necessary part of the family." Marriage and family have long been considered civilizing influences on young men. Whether or not causation can be proven, it is true that unwed fathers are more likely to use drugs and become involved in criminal behavior than are other men.

Replacing Welfare with Private Charity

The 1996 welfare reforms were a step in the right direction, but much more needs to be done. The next step should be to transfer full responsibility for funding and administering welfare programs to the states. The states would have freedom to innovate with their low-income programs and would have strong incentives to reduce taxpayer costs and maximize work incentives.

The ultimate reform goal, however, should be to eliminate the entire system of low-income welfare for individuals who are able to work. That means eliminating not just TANF but also food stamps, subsidized housing, and other programs. Individuals unwilling to support themselves through the job market would have to rely on the support of family, church, community, or private charity.

What would happen to the poor if welfare were eliminated? Without the negative incentives created by the welfare state, fewer people would be poor. There would also likely be fewer children born into poverty. Studies suggest that women do make rational decisions about whether to have children, and thus a reduction in welfare benefits would reduce the likelihood of their becoming pregnant or having children out of wedlock.

In addition, some poor women who had children out of wedlock would put the children up for adoption. The government should encourage that by eliminating the present regulatory and bureaucratic barriers to adoption. Other unmarried women who gave birth would not be able to afford to live independently and they would have to live with their families or boyfriends. Some would choose to marry the fathers of their children.

Despite the positive social effects of ending government welfare, there will still be many people who make mistakes and find themselves in tough situations. Americans are an enormously generous people, and there is a vast amount of private charitable support available, especially for people truly in need.

Private charity is superior to government welfare for many reasons. Private charities are able to individualize their approaches to the circumstances of poor people. By contrast, government programs are usually designed in a one-size-fits-all manner that treats all recipients alike. Most government programs rely on the simple provision of cash or services without any attempt to differentiate between the needs of recipients.

The eligibility requirements for government welfare programs are arbitrary and cannot be changed to fit individual circumstances. Consequently, some people in genuine need do not receive assistance, while benefits often go to people who do not really need them. Surveys of people with low incomes generally indicate a higher level of satisfaction with private charities than with government welfare agencies.

Private charities also have a better record of actually delivering aid to recipients because they do not have as much administrative overhead, inefficiency, and waste as government programs. A lot of the money spent on federal and state social welfare programs never reaches recipients because it is consumed by fraud and bureaucracy.

Audits of TANF spending by the Health and Human Services' Inspector General have found huge levels of "improper payments," meaning errors, abuse, and fraud. In 2005, the state of New York had an improper TANF payment rate of 28 percent and Michigan had an improper payment rate of 40 percent. During 2006 and 2007, Ohio had an improper payment rate in TANF of 21 percent. There are similar high levels of waste in other states.

Another advantage of private charity is that aid is much more likely to be targeted to short-term emergency assistance, not long-term dependency. Private charity provides a safety net, not a way of life. Moreover, private charities may demand that the poor change their behavior in exchange for assistance, such as stopping drug abuse, looking for a job, or avoiding pregnancy. Private charities are more likely than government programs to offer counseling and one-on-one follow-up, rather than simply providing a check.

In sum, private charities typically require a different attitude on the part of recipients. They are required to consider the aid they receive not as an entitlement, but as a gift carrying reciprocal obligations. At the same time, private charities require that donors become directly involved in monitoring program performance.

Government Welfare Crowds Out Charitable Activities

Those who oppose replacing government welfare with private charity often argue that there will not be enough charitable giving to make up for the loss of government benefits. However, that assumes that private charity would simply recreate existing government programs. But the advantage of private and decentralized charity is that less expensive and more innovative ways of helping smaller groups of truly needy people would be developed.

If large amounts of aid continue to be needed, there is every reason to believe that charitable giving in the nation would increase in the absence of government welfare. In every area of society and the economy, we have seen that government expansion tends to "crowd out" private voluntary activities. So, in reverse, when the government shrinks, private activities would fill in the gaps.

A number of studies have demonstrated such a government crowd-out effect in low-income assistance. Charitable giving declined dramatically during the 1970s, as the Great Society programs of the 1960s were expanding. The decline in giving leveled out in the 1980s as welfare spending began to level out and the public was deluged with news stories about supposed cutbacks in federal programs. Then, after the passage of welfare reform in 1996, there was a large spike in private giving. Studies have also shown that when particular charities start receiving government funds, there is a decrease in private donations to those charities.

Americans are the most generous people on earth, contributing more than $300 billion a year to organized private charities. In addition, they volunteer more than 8 billion hours a year to charitable activities, with an estimated value of about $158 billion. Americans donate countless dollars and countless efforts toward providing informal help to families, neighbors, and others in need. There is every reason to believe that the elimination of government welfare would bring a very positive response both from recipients of government welfare and from Americans wanting to help those who are truly in need.

Organizations to Contact

*The editors have compiled the following list of organizations con-
cerned with the issues debated in this book. The descriptions are
derived from materials provided by the organizations. All have
publications or information available for interested readers. The
list was compiled on the date of publication of the present volume;
the information provided here may change. Be aware that many
organizations take several weeks or longer to respond to inquiries,
so allow as much time as possible.*

Advocates for Youth

2000 M Street NW, Suite 750
Washington, DC 20036
(202) 419-3420 • fax: (202) 419-1448
website: www.advocatesforyouth.org

Advocates for Youth is a national organization seeking to provide
young people with adequate information to enable them to make
educated decisions about their reproductive and sexual health.
The organization focuses its efforts on promoting three main values: rights, respect, and responsibility. The site provides detailed
information about teen pregnancy prevention including general
facts and racial and ethnic disparities in teen pregnancy rates.
The site also provides information about the National Support
Center for State Teen Pregnancy Prevention Organizations,
which helps state programs provide teens with effective resources
concerning teen pregnancy and sexually transmitted infections.

American Civil Liberties Union (ACLU)

125 Broad Street, 18th Floor
New York, NY 10004
website: www.aclu.org

The ACLU is a national civil rights organization dedicated to protecting the civil liberties guaranteed to all Americans under the US Constitution, including first amendment rights, equal protection, due process, and privacy. Much of the organization's work focuses on historically underserved groups, and as such, teen pregnancy and teen parents' rights have been the topic of much of their work. Specifically the ACLU has tackled teen parents' right to education and bullying against teen parents in schools. Details about cases taken by the organization, along with articles and commentary, can be read on the ACLU website.

Centers for Disease Control and Prevention (CDC)

1600 Clifton Road
Atlanta, GA 30333
(800) CDC-INFO
website: www.cdc.gov

The CDC is the national agency charged with ensuring the continued health and safety of US citizens. In addition to tackling diseases, the CDC determines the general health of the nation from a variety of perspectives. Teen pregnancy falls among these areas. Statistics, information about teen pregnancy prevention, and social media tools can be accessed on the CDC website under the heading Teen Pregnancy.

Children's Aid Society (CAS)

105 East 22nd Street
New York, NY 10010
(212) 949-4800
website: www.childrensaidsociety.org

CAS works to ensure that children in poverty have the opportunity to live happy, healthy lives and achieve their goals. While the organization primarily focuses on the health and well-being of children, CAS developed the Carrera Adolescent Sexuality and Pregnancy Prevention Program, which has been used or copied in some form in nearly half the states in the country. Detailed information about this program can be found on the CAS Carrera Adolescent Pregnancy Prevention website.

Healthy Teen Network (HTN)

1501 Saint Paul Street, Suite 124
Baltimore, MD 21202
(410) 685-0410 • fax: (410) 685-0481
website: www.healthyteennetwork.org

HTN works on a national level to provide support and educational resources—focusing on teen pregnancy prevention, teen pregnancy, and teen parenting—to reproductive health care professionals across the country. The main strategies implemented by the organization are network and information sharing, research and program evaluation, training and technical assistance, organizational and coalition capacity building, and policy and advocacy. Publications and resources about teen pregnancy derived from these approaches can be accessed on the HTN website.

Mothers Helping Mothers Inc.

1393 E. Broad Street, Floor 2, #224
Columbus, OH 43205
(877) 858-8890
e-mail: mhmsinc1@gmail.com
website: www.mhmteen.org

Mothers Helping Mothers Inc. is a nonprofit organization that supports pregnant teens and young mothers by helping them develop life skills that are crucial to raising a family. By empowering young mothers through mentoring and education, the organization gives young women the ability to become independent and achieve their goals. The organization's website includes information on current projects as well as links to resources for young mothers and anyone who would like to get involved with the program.

National Campaign to Prevent Teen and Unplanned Pregnancy
1776 Massachusetts Avenue NW, Suite 200
Washington, DC 20036
(202) 478-8500 • fax: (202) 478-8588
website: www.thenationalcampaign.org

Since 1996, the National Campaign to Prevent Teen and Unplanned Pregnancy has sought to reduce the rates of teen and unplanned pregnancy in the United States. This organization provides national and state data on both of these topics along with extensive resources on topics ranging from contraception access to public policy and sex education.

National Center on Fathers and Families (NCOFF)
3440 Market Street, Suite 450
Philadelphia, PA 19104
(215) 573-5500
website: www.ncoff.gse.upenn.edu

NCOFF has been working since 1994 to conduct research and develop practices that increase the information available on the impact of fathers' involvement and family development on children and families. This information is also used to help create policies that make children's lives better. Documents available on the NCOFF website include father figure facts and a variety of publications detailing research findings and policy suggestions.

National Women's Law Center (NWLC)
11 Dupont Circle NW, #800
Washington, DC 20036
(202) 588-5180
e-mail: info@nwlc.org
website: www.nwlc.org

NWLC works to ensure that women and girls in the United States have a wide range of opportunities to live productive, happy lives. The primary issues of focus are education, employment, family and economic security, and health and reproductive rights. In accordance with these topics, teen pregnancy has been researched and written about extensively, particularly with respect to teen moms' education rights. Articles such as "Title IX: A Promise Not Yet Fulfilled" and "It's Not Just About Sports . . . The Rights of Pregnant and Parenting Students under Title IX" can be read on the NWLC website.

National Youth Rights Association (NYRA)
1101 15th Street NW, Suite 200
Washington, DC 20005
(202) 835-1739
website: www.youthrights.org

The National Youth Rights Association is a youth-led national nonprofit organization dedicated to fighting for the civil rights and liberties of young people. NYRA has more than seven thousand members representing all fifty states. It seeks to lower the voting age, lower the drinking age, repeal curfew laws, and protect student rights.

Office of Adolescent Health (OAH)
1101 Wootton Parkway, Suite 700
Rockville, MD 20852
(240) 453-2846
e-mail: oah.gov@hhs.gov
website: www.hhs.gov

OAH is an office within the US Department of Health and Human Services that seeks to promote healthy living for adolescents when they are young so they are able to grow into healthy adults. Among the wide range of programs administered by the office are research and implementation of teen pregnancy prevention programs and the Pregnancy Assistance Fund. The OAH website provides details about both of these programs.

YoungLives

PO Box 520
Colorado Springs, CO 80901
(877) 438-9572 • fax: (719) 381-1750
website: www.younglife.org/younglives

YoungLives is a Christian ministry, within the larger youth ministry Young Life, dedicated specifically to reaching teen mothers and providing them with love, respect, support, and parenting advice. Through its mentoring and camping programs, this organization provides young mothers a place they can turn to for assistance. Information about organization programs as well as regional contacts can be found on the YoungLives website.

A Young Mother's D.R.E.A.M.

46 East 57th Street
Brooklyn, NY 11203
(646) 481-1693
e-mail: info@youngmothersdream.org
website: www.youngmothersdream.org

A Young Mother's D.R.E.A.M. is a nonprofit organization dedicated to helping mothers between the ages of sixteen and twenty-three attain an education with the assistance of a mentor who was also a young mother. As part of this program, the pairs attend workshops that promote healthy choices, goal setting, and education. Additionally, the teens have the opportunity to participate in a radio show to discuss the issues that they face as young mothers. Information on these programs and additional resources can be found on the organization's website.

For Further Reading

Books

Robert Coles, *The Youngest Parents.* New York: Norton, 2000.

Lisa Covitch, *The Epidemic of Teen Pregnancy: An American Tragedy.* Pittsburgh, PA: RoseDog, 2012.

Deborah Davis, ed., *You Look Too Young to Be a Mom: Teen Mothers on Love, Learning, and Success.* New York: Perigee, 2004.

Letizia Guglielmo, *MTV and Teen Pregnancy: Critical Essays on 16 and Pregnant and Teen Mom.* Lanham, MD: Scarecrow, 2013.

Saul D. Hoffman and Rebecca A. Maynard, eds., *Kids Having Kids: Economic Costs and Social Consequences of Teen Pregnancy.* Washington, DC: Urban Institute, 2008.

Evelyn Lerman, *Teen Moms: The Pain and the Promise.* Buena Park, CA: Morning Glory, 1997.

Jeanne Warren Lindsay, *Teen Dads: Rights, Responsibilities and Joys.* Buena Park, CA: Morning Glory, 2008.

Jeanne Warren Lindsay and Jean Brunelli, *Your Pregnancy and Newborn Journey: A Guide for Pregnant Teens.* Buena Park, CA: Morning Glory, 2004.

Kristin Luker, *Dubious Conceptions: The Politics of Teenage Pregnancy.* Cambridge, MA: Harvard University Press, 1997.

Gaby Rodriguez with Jenna Glatzer, *The Pregnancy Project: A Memoir.* New York: Simon & Schuster, 2012.

Dorrie Williams-Wheeler, *The Unplanned Pregnancy Book for Teens and College Students.* Virginia Beach, VA: Sparkledoll, 2004.

James Wong and David Checkland, eds., *Teen Pregnancy and Parenting: Social and Ethical Issues.* Toronto, ON: University of Toronto Press, 1999.

Periodicals

Charletta Dillard and Kenya N. Byrd, "Beating the Odds," *Jet,* August 1, 2011.

Economist, "Setting Aside Childish Things," July 28, 2012.

Sarah Ferris, "Curbing Teen Births," *Governing,* December 2012.

Megan Foreman, "Taking Responsibility," *State Legislatures,* February 2011.

Sheila Gibbons, "Teen Pregnancy 'Pact' Sparks Media Frenzy— But They Miss the Story," *Media Report to Women,* Summer 2008.

Kathy Gulli et al., "Suddenly Teen Pregnancy Is Cool?," *Maclean's,* January 28, 2008.

Marina Khidekel, "Could Hollywood Trick You into Getting Pregnant?," *Seventeen,* May 2010.

Christine Kim and Robert E. Rector, "The Joy of Abstaining," *USA Today,* March 2009.

Molly Lopez et al., "Growing up Too Fast," *People,* January 14, 2008.

Todd Melby, "New Study Explains Rise in Teen Birth Rate," *Contemporary Sexuality,* August 2010.

Nancy Redd, "Pregnant on Purpose," *Cosmo Girl,* August 2008.

Denise Rinaldo, "The Tough Life of a Teen Mom," *Scholastic Choices,* January 2012.

Nirvi Shah, "Title IX Falls Short of Promise for Pregnant Students," *Education Week,* June 13, 2012.

Margaret Talbot, "Red Sex, Blue Sex," *New Yorker*, November 3, 2008.

Chandra R. Thomas, "Memphis Schools Set Record Straight on Student Pregnancies," *Jet*, April 4, 2011.

Jennifer Van Pelt, "Keeping Teen Moms in School," *Social Work Today*, March–April 2012.

Kelly White, "When You Least Expect It," *Girls' Life*, February/March 2008.

Index